ROBIN BANKSY

Robin Barton

A MEMOIR

A tale of two Robins

dedicated to Banksy

CONTENTS

01. WHAT	1
02. SUCCESS	7
03. ARBITRAGE	13
04. POLICE AND THIEVES	19
05. PERIHELION	25
06. MOSSACK FONSECA	31
07. Y2K	37
08. MY DADDY WAS A BANKROBBER	43
09. GYPSIES TRAMPS AND THIEVES	49
10. PRICK	61
11. DO YOU KNOW WHO I AM	67
12. PEST CONTROL	73
13. VERMIN	77
14. THE BUTCHER OF BETHLEHEM	81
15. MONTAUK	89
16. GOODNIGHT IRENE	95
17. AFTER IRENE	101
18. SLAVE LABOUR	107
19. LITTLE HOUSE	115
20. THIEVES LIKE US	121
21. NO BALL GAMES	127
22. SHEPHERD MARKET	137
23. GIRL WITH BALLOON	149
24. KARMA POLICE	157
25. Q	167
26. ART BUFF	173
27. MIAMI VICE	181
28. DREAMLAND	187
29. COMPLIANCE	193
30. WHEN WE WERE KINGS	201
31. I'M GOING TO TEAR YOUR PLAYHOUSE DOWN	209
32. EPILOGUE	219
33. SHIP OF FOOLS	225
34. A FOOL AND HIS MONEY	233
35. SHOP 'TIL YOU DROP	243

WHAT

WHAT

It is London, December 2007, and I am stood in front of the city's most celebrated and influential PR guru, to each side his deliberate and silent foot soldiers hanging on his every word, and the words being uttered on this dark December evening are simple and measured in tone, "Tell me why I should buy this work." I prepare to roll out my much practised pitch, the game changer, the art bullshit. But instead I falter, hesitate and turn theatrically to point at six crudely stencilled letters that read...

BANKSY

The feral boy child featured, is angrily brandishing a large paintbrush having recently daubed the word 'WHAT?' to the painting's steel canvas. Now glaring straight past me and defiantly into the eyes of the captive audience of three. Six random letters that were to define the coming decade... The die cast, the hand dealt.

[WHAT?] Stencil & Spray Paint on 6mm steel - Sold £250,000.

London, December 1987, twenty years earlier, and I am walking through the doors of 72-74 Brewer Street, Soho, the headquarters of MCA Records. And on following the stairs up to a small fourth floor office I find myself in the presence of their newly appointed PR wunderkind, his determined and youthful exuberance giving him the air of someone who knew his time was now and whose energy clearly transgressed the usual lumbering and leaden pace of the music industry of the period. One that had grown fat and lazy over two decades of excessive and extravagant gesture, a bloated top-heavy business that had found itself arriving inappropriately dressed and hopelessly late to the very party it believed it was hosting.

But this wunderkind was about to jolt it out of its torpor and I was an eager and willing passenger to his plans. Less than 48 hours later I'm sitting in the first class lounge of a British Airways Boeing 747 taxiing toward Terminal 7, Gate No.3 of New York's John F. Kennedy International Airport. I was there to cover the stateside tour of the bafflingly popular British band 'The Fixx'. Having finally cleared immigration following a number of urgent (and to my mind entirely unnecessary) calls back to London's MCA offices regarding my 'Countenance', I was politely and patiently bundled into the rear of a preposterously ostentatious black Lincoln Continental limousine that had been tasked to deliver me to the Gramercy Park Hotel sited just a twenty minute ride from the twin towers of the city's World Trade Center.

I am twenty-seven years old, have never previously left England. I am elated and really very drunk.

In that same month actor Michael Douglas's character Gordon Gekko had declared without guilt or guile that "Greed is Good", an assertion that had marked a cultural shift from post-war apology to the enthusiastic embrace of corporate greed. Whilst Orwell had been wrong and there had been no 'Big Brother' or adoption of a totalitarian state, something equally profound had taken grip of the psyche of an increasingly anxious society. In early 1987 Motorola had released its first commercial mobile phone. The DynaTAC 8000X, a handset that had offered 30 minutes of talk-time, six hours standby, and could store 30 phone numbers. The cost - £2,639. Later that same year its Finnish competitor Nokia had launched the Mobira Cityman 900 with a handset that offered 50 minutes talk-time, fourteen hours standby at a cost of just £1,950. And when photographs of the progressive Soviet leader Mikhail Gorbachev using a Cityman to make a call from Helsinki to Moscow were beamed across the globe, it became an overnight sensation, an iconic emblem of wealth and success, a salute to a new era of connectivity, one that eschewed and ignored the rigours and restrictions of the Soviet regime's Iron Curtain. The genie was out of the bottle and everything had changed.

Back on the other side of the Atlantic and seven years on from the release of the prophetic The Long Good Friday, I had found myself in the company of the then Prime Minister Margaret Thatcher along with the famously reclusive billionaire businessman Paul Reichmann, who had unwittingly picked up the fictional baton held out by the film's central character, a steely psychotic gangster played by the actor Bob Hoskins, whose Harold 'Harry' Shand had naively and unsuccessfully courted members of a sceptical and dangerous American Mafia to help fund his dream - a visionary reimagining of the broken-down and abandoned docks that littered the island's foreshore. As we stood on that same desolate stretch of wasteland that bordered the northern edge of the Isle of Dogs, I felt I could sense the psychic echo of his anguished disappointment and betrayal hanging in the air all about me. I was there to record the laying of the cornerstone of the wildly ambitious One Canada Square, a gleaming tower of Babel that was set to be the zenith of a new financial district, a beacon to a New World Order where money would become our master. A single shining edifice that on completion would forever eviscerate the ink stained soul of Fleet Street, for the first time in London's history making bedfellows of an international press and a burgeoning financial industry. A calamitous and uncomfortable pairing that would send ripples of discontent and deceit throughout the city for decades to come.

Four years later and I'm riding the elevator to the 15th floor of the newly completed One Canada Square for the Daily Telegraph's first Christmas party at their newly appointed offices, a newspaper that only three years earlier reported on a systemic and seismic shock, which had rocked the city to its core culminating in what became known as Black Monday, a day that marked a historic global stock market crash, a deregulated financial market that had spiralled out of control creating a 'New City Army' formed of brash young men hungry for success, replacing the grey post-war, bowler-hatted gentlemen, whose mannered ebb and flow across its city's bridges had marked each trading day with metronomic regularity for decades. This new breed of 'Jobbers and Brokers' strutted aggressively like pit-cocks. Puffed up with adrenalin they carried with them an ugly arrogance and swagger that spilled out from the trading floors into the pubs and bars of an increasingly avaricious city, the chalk boards of the nearby Bleeding Heart Yard echoed and amplified the madness with evermore extravagant offers. 'Happy hours' became 'happy nights'. Champagne flowed like water. Trading volumes jumped within a single week from $4.5 billion to a dazzling $7.4 billion. The 'Big Bang' had arrived and there seemed to be no limit to its excess, creating in its wake more than 1,500 new millionaires.

It hadn't made a millionaire of me but I had enthusiastically adopted its '3C' diet - Coffee, Cocaine and Champagne.

SUCCESS

SUCCESS

Number 29 Pembroke Gardens was a handsome late-Victorian townhouse, whose tessellated and brightly polished steps rose steeply from the pavement to a sturdy, smartly dressed ebony black door that emanated a reassuring air of sobriety and success. But 'below stairs' told of a very different story.

Accessed by a somewhat truncated and cobweb-strewn door the basement flat, with its oppressively low ceilings and limited daylight, pointed to the accommodation having been clearly designed as staff quarters, within which every expense had been spared. Any light that did make the perilous journey down its narrow stone steps had been further dimmed by the introduction of solid prison-like bars to its windows, described by the neurotic and wary landlord as a 'necessary' security precaution. But to anyone who harboured the slightest fear of felonious retribution, it had reeked of incarceration.

Importantly, sited within the confines of its dingy dark hallway had been installed, a temperamental and fiercely greedy payphone whose insatiable appetite was significantly larger than that of its steel-lined stomach. It had required regular emptying by its miserly key-holder, who would routinely descend uninvited, from 'above stairs', his rattling chain of keys like Jacob Marley's ghost announcing his arrival. But in the pre-mobile age of the period it had represented a vital lifeline and critical to my advancement. Its number began with the all important '07' prefix - the gold standard of London telecommunications, a prefixed line-number that announced you were in the game, ready for action, awaiting the clarion call to arms.

For all the disadvantages and inconveniences of this subterranean silo, it held an ace in its hand. In the no-doubt light-filled high-ceilinged rooms of the raised ground floor above, had resided the actor Martin Shaw, one half of the fictional duo in the hit television series The Professionals. This alone had given me hope in adversity and I had convinced myself that my current state of penury was a fleeting aberration which, with a little attention and a fair wind, could and would be corrected. The caché of celebrity must surely find its way down the forlorn and forsaken steps to knock at my door. To invite itself in, share a drink and raise a toast.

Each Friday morning during those early years, I had set out on the onerous and arduous journey to the gulag-like dole offices of Lisson Grove for the weekly humiliation afforded me by its mean-spirited and cruel subjugators. On my way I would take time to marvel at the grandeur and decadence of the villas that edged the southern borders of Holland Park. Lord Leighton's opulent opium-inspired palace, film director and 'grand viveur' Michael Winner's gleaming stable of supercars paraded and perfect in the park's morning light. Then on to stand and stare in awe and envy at the magnificent and malevolent 'The Tower House', a gothic revival masterpiece that had been home to amongst its number the Hollywood heartthrob James Mason, starman David Bowie, the occultist and outsider Aleister Crowley and more recently the hellraiser Richard Harris, who at the tender age of just twenty four, following a hard night's drinking, had awoken on its lawn to declare that he would one day be its owner.

Its current owner being the founder and frontman of the legendary rock band Led Zeppelin, his very own house of the holy with its own private stairway to heaven. A house that to my mind represented the very zenith of success, a dark brooding fortress promising sanctuary against the mundanities of daily rigour. I had imagined myself at some future point, cocooned in its inner sanctum, moving majestically from room to room swathed in exotic velvets and silk, surrounded by its mystical murals whilst sharing riotous tales of hedonistic excess in the company of its spectral forebears. I had convinced myself that sheer willpower alone could and would be enough to make this imagining real. That it remained out of reach for now was a mere trifle, an inconvenience to be dealt with on another day.

Returning from these weekly excursions and with a soft sun setting to the west, the artist David Hockney could often be seen pottering about his courtyard at Pembroke Studios opposite. Across the nearby Edwardes Square as the shutters of the local Scarsdale Tavern were finally pulled shut, the veteran comedian Frankie Howerd could be heard loudly and drunkenly regaling the neighbourhood with his lewd and extravagant late night outpourings, as he edged his way cautiously and clumsily around the square toward his home. There he'd be met nightly by his hapless and patient housekeeper who would coax and cajole him in off the street to the searing and sardonic applause of his closest neighbours. On another occasion across from the Earls Court police station I had caught sight of a preening and picture perfect Brian Ferry, checking his reflection in the security mirror of the local corner shop before purchasing a packet of cigarettes and disappearing suavely into the night. I had felt sure that the planets were aligning themselves in my favour and the tides of fortune were turning my way, beckoning me on enthusiastically.

Throughout the eighties and nineties, as twilight approached, the windows of Freddie Mercury's high walled Garden Lodge mansion had twinkled exotically with eastern promise. George Michael had taken up residence in the nearby Adam and Eve mews. The HIV Aids crisis that had threatened to extinguish all joy from the city, whilst not having gone away, had seemed somehow more abstract and remote. The decade bookended by Bob Geldof's 'Band Aid' and 'Band Aid II' rolled seamlessly into the nineties with a youthful and energetic swagger.

For my part I had fashioned an illusion, one conjured of smoke and mirrors, a paper-thin pretence, an ominous portent that had I paid it heed, might have stopped me in my tracks. But the arrogance of youth had filtered out any underlying doubt. It was to be the first of many lies that were to shape and inform my future. I had determined to make a success of myself at any cost and if artifice and invention were to be my allies along the way so be it.

It would be a further five years before a young Bristolian would pack together a few meagre possessions, some half-empty spray cans and rolls of old stencil paper and set out on the one-hundred-mile journey from the rural backwater of his youth to the gold-paved streets of London Town in search of fame and fortune.

ARBITRAGE

ARBITRAGE

On the night of 15th October 1987, a violent extratropical cyclone born of a severe depression had swept eastward off the Bay of Biscay wreaking havoc across vast swathes of the country, causing damage in excess of £2 billion. I had been less than a month away from turning 30 years old and I am fighting my own depression. Having unexpectedly lost my foothold in Kensington proper following an unfortunate drinking incident, I had been forced to migrate to the bleak and brutish northern reaches of the borough. Settling on a multi-occupied, single-bathroomed rathole that was home to a transient group of damaged and dissolute drinkers, who attracted by its proximity to the 'The Eagle' pub adjacent, came and went with the tides of misfortune and malaise. In truth a perfect hiding place for a thirsty adventurer of my stature. Not 'The Tower House' of my dreams but it was early on my journey and I had a way to go yet.

Opening the front door of 273 Ladbroke Grove the next morning, I had been met by the surreal vision of more than a dozen mature London plane trees lying across the road like so many giant collapsed drunks, their canopy of branches pushing through the stone balustrades and railings of the surrounding houses. Having slept through that night, I was blissfully unaware of the 100mph winds that had angrily charged across Holland Park, devastating its tranquil calm, rushing North past the Ladbroke Grove police station and pushing violently under the concrete arm of the Westway where six weeks earlier the Notting Hill Carnival had been witness to the mindless stabbing of 23-year-old stall holder Michael Galvin, on past the 7-Eleven convenience store and the legendary Dub Vendor

Reggae Shack then further northward, briefly but unsuccessfully attempting to wake me from my drink induced stupor. There had been menace in the air all that year, It seemed a rapacious avarice had taken hold of the city, pulsing out from the trading floors like a cancer. The comic Harry Enfield's openly ironic character, aimed at lampooning these grotesques, had instead become a badge of honour, one adopted by packs of drunken young men aggressively shouting 'Loadsamoney' whilst waving wads of notes into the air, their ruddy faces matched only by the crimson braces that identified their tribe.

Over that Saturday and Sunday as the clean up from what had become known as the 'Great Storm' began in earnest, across town a quite separate and silent storm was brewing. Not this time over the Bay of Biscay but within the seemingly inert humming mainframe computers, the 'Big Irons' that slumbered restlessly, awaiting the surge of activity that would mark the start of a new trading week. But it was on this Monday, of this year, that an unprecedented number of trades had overwhelmed its own computers and communications systems and was literally choking itself. Unfilled orders sat in limbo, large fund transfers languished for hours in no man's land, causing consternation and confusion.

By the end of the trading day the invincible had become vulnerable and a global tidal wave had swept through the markets leaving a tideline of wrecked lives and shattered dreams. The vulgar reckless freewheeling fast-living lifestyle, which had defined the twelve-month period between the 'Big Bang' and 'Black Monday' would never fully return and the city foot soldiers with their boorish and uncouth behavior had been called abruptly to book.

The party was over and open outcry trading was gradually phased out in favour of new and improved electronic, screen-based trading systems. That enabled faster, cheaper and less error-prone trades. The frenzied baying and bullying of these outdated trading pits had fallen silent, a moribund relic slain by the relentless progress of technology.

A new dawn had broken over the city, each morning a snaking convoy of rasping silver, black and grey Porsches sped across the city's bridges that served as the arteries to a freshly resuscitated beating heart, one engorged on global greed. Everything was coded, every action a purposeful show of strength. The cartoonish excess of those pioneer traders was over. 'Loadsamoney' replaced by a colder, more ruthless and unscrupulous breed. Sharp-suited speculators focused on accumulating vast sums that moved silently and seamlessly throughout the newly installed networks. With the estimated 1,500 millionaires thought to had been created as a result of Prime Minister Thatcher's city deregulation, a new breed of spender had been born.

Young and unencumbered by class guilt, they were eager to parade their newly acquired status and wealth. Watches, cars, real estate and international travel became the new symbols of success. Money was viewed with callous disregard, stealth-like black credit cards replacing the previously brandished fists of cash. Newton's third law dictates that with every action there is an equal and opposite reaction. The unintended consequence of the astonishing advance of technology was that complex data trails were being laid, millions of trades logged in a web of electronic memory. The unregulated wild west had been tamed and its cowboys lassoed by their own avarice. Debarred and dangerous these natural predators sought new hunting grounds and a small but significant number settled upon a tired and fusty industry. If arbitrage could be applied unchallenged to an increasingly regulated market, then it was logical that it could be applied with equal if not greater success to one without regulation.

[Arbitrage] the simultaneous purchase and sale of an asset to profit from an imbalance in its price.

POLICE AND THIEVES

POLICE AND THIEVES

Art, crime and commerce have long been close bedfellows. Tracing back as far as the famously powerful and corrupt Medici family, the Italian banking dynasty whose fervent patronage and power had propelled Michelangelo to superstardom. Pope makers and breakers, they had set the gold standard, one that has been replicated throughout history from the Rothschilds, through to the Rockefellers and the Gettys - dynasties who had both supported (and hoarded) the spoils of artistic endeavour as a form of self-gratification and aggrandisement.

It's the evening of March 13th, 1990, I'm steadying myself against Jack Leach's black 1968 Roll's Royce Cornice Convertible, urinating fiercely and distractedly as Jack, seemingly unconcerned by my aim, is regaling me with the story of how he had purchased the car from the British actor Michael Caine. This particular model it transpired had rolled off the production line when I was just ten years old.

Jack was the legendary proprietor of the wonderfully eccentric and notorious Gasworks restaurant, an institution sited at an indefinable location, somewhere deep in South West London's hinterland, between Chelsea's World's End and the industrial wastelands of Fulham. It was by many reckoned to be the last true vestige of the swinging sixties, a place where royalty, rogues and rock stars could leave their cloaks, coats and capes at the door and indulge in carefully curated courtships. Amongst its number could be counted Princess Margaret, the gangster John Bindon and various members of the Rolling Stones to name but a few. Often times you could find yourself sharing council with an errant lord or failed aristocrat, but just as likely and without ceremony, you could find yourself sat next to a recent release from one of Her Majesty's Prisons sporting little more than a black bin liner of possessions. Jack was nothing if not magnanimous, both in spirit and soul, and if your tolerance did not match his you would not get through the door. Once through that door you had entered a theatre of the absurd, its cast apparently trapped in a timeless dress rehearsal. Democratically non-judgemental of their audience's excesses and indiscretions, content to share in their troupe's secrets and proclivities on a nightly basis.

The restaurants main dining room was a lavishly and provocatively festooned stage set, with erotica applied to every surface, dark alcoves home to dissolute busts and crumbling taxidermy and in one corner sat atop a marble table stood a large, proudly pornographic chess set with its engorged pawns, boastfully fecund kings and derelict knaves. Then there was 'Shells' who dominated the restaurants cramped kitchen, a chaotic and wildly opinionated women, whose severe and long-standing agoraphobia had rendered her all but incapable of understanding that there even existed a world outside her immediate environs. Conversations with her would veer helter-skelter like through history, and without the anchor of time to give context, were always bewildering oblique, disarmingly frank and often gloriously vulgar. Fag in mouth she would prod and poke at the trays of murdered creatures that made up that nights offering.

The menu (like the rest of this theatre's set) had, I suspected, remained largely unchanged since its first night. There was 'Duck' and there was 'Lamb' and neither dish bore any resemblance to their title. Each night, to the long polished-marble table, surrounded by solid high-backed chairs, the anomalous offerings would be delivered with studied reverence by the fabulously louche 'Pearl'.

A young, effete, weasel-thin soul - variously described as Shell's son and or her lover, he carried with him the beleaguered air of someone who had seen everything just one too many times.

Throughout each night's production Jack would regularly and remorselessly chide him with a menacing yet choreographed zeal that kept diners on the edge of their seats. Only when the candles were snuffed out and the audience had emptied drunkenly into another Chelsea dawn did you get the sense that you had borne witness to a lovingly and sincerely-meant portrait of an era whose players knew only too well was slipping through the hands of history, an era whose run was perilously close to its end.

If the Gasworks represented the last bastion of a vanishing age, then all around me were appearing further portents and cracks in the fabric. For me the decade that had become pluralised as the noughties had been one of excess and half rememberings. I had physically bumped into Francis Bacon just a year before his death as he had lurched myopically out from the entrance of Barker's Arcade sited at the top of Kensington High Street, dressed in faded gold corduroys, a livid purple leather jacket and mustard roll neck. His face like a large ruddy dinner plate had momentarily stared back at me then blinked owl-like and melancholic before vanishing back into the crowd.

Nightly I had walked past Lucien Freud's manager's office, situated in a handsome Victorian townhouse located at the northern reach of Kensington Church Street, its windows occasioning glimpses of his prodigy's most recent endeavours. Returning from my nocturnal wanderings, I had often caught sight of their creator, sailing sleuth-like between assignations, criss-crossing the streets and mews of West London behind the wheel of his faded ochre-coloured Bentley Mk VI, the very same model purchased by Ian Fleming's James Bond in his 1955 novel, Moonraker.

The superstar artist had yet to be invented but for now there had existed just a small group of dissolute outsiders made up of gamblers, drunks and philanderers who seemingly held money in scant regard. This tight-knit group of émigrés and outcasts had revelled in the post-war sleaze of London's Soho, with its clip-joints, dive bars and members' clubs, burning through the spoils of their labours extravagantly and without care. It was to this London that I had been attracted, its tales and imagery acting as a mesmeric and magnetic lure, promising sexual adventure and drunken excess. One that I had snatched with pike-like enthusiasm, content to be reeled in from the dull and shallow constraints of the Midlands town of my birth.

By the time I had arrived at their West London playground, they were no longer young men and their reputation that had burned so brightly was already fading. But I had felt grateful and excited to be breathing in the same air and to be walking those same hallowed streets. I had set out to make my own story but I was determined to learn from my mentors and had applied myself to the onerous and exhaustive task in hand, enthusiastically and tirelessly working my way through the pubs and clubs of eighties Soho.

A typical day might start with a restorative beer at the Nell Gwynne Tavern just off the Strand, situated in the gloriously atmospheric Bull Inn Court, a shadowy urine-drenched passageway that runs north to the southern borders of Covent Garden. Its proximity and near invisibility providing sanctuary to generations of cast and crew from the nearby Adelphi, Vaudeville and Savoy theatres. Shouldering past the bodach and spectres that inhabited this dark void, then on to Bradleys Spanish Bar located at the southernmost end of Hanway Street, a dark venal thoroughfare littered with illegal drinking dens, connecting Tottenham Court Road to Oxford Street with no apparent purpose other than to steal your money and time. Bradleys' owner, a swarthy gold-toothed sovereign-ringed mountain of a man, had policed his tiny empire with a zeal and vigour matched only by that of his extraordinary tan - rumoured to have been acquired whilst avoiding extradition from the Costa Del Sol on various and colourful counts of criminality.

Then on, to the cramped cave-like basement of the St Moritz Club on Wardour Street, perhaps diverting to the French House to marvel at its host Gaston's extravagant moustache and to revel in the many tales of his bar's role in La Résistance. Zigzagging greedily between Blacks, the Gargoyle and the Groucho on Dean Street, finally landing chaotically into the fluorescent livid-green interior of the Colony Room for an entirely unnecessary night cap that would invariably and inevitably continue until the Soho skyline had begun its daily reveal. Struggling back to my Kensington basement to sleep, only to start over again the next day.

The consequence of this adopted lifestyle was not without jeopardy. On one occasion, I'd found myself sat with a friend, basking in the privilege of a local West London 'lock-in' when the pub's door had been urgently and abruptly kicked open followed by three armed balaclavaed men. We had sat statue-still as we watched two of the men violently bundle the shocked and shaken staff up the pub's stairway to where presumably they thought the safe might be located. The third man, recognising an opportunity, had swiftly stepped behind the bar, removed his balaclava and poured himself a pint.

Turning to survey the lounge, he was forced to reconcile the sight of two stock-still silent drinkers, doing their level best to not exist. For the briefest of moments the three of us, pints in hand, might have appeared to resemble little more than a regular London pub scene on any given night - a notion that belied the violent adrenalin-soaked atmosphere we were actually experiencing.

There then followed a farcical scene, wherein the gunman in his haste to conceal his identity had pulled his balaclava back over his face, only this time, back to front, rendering him all but blind to the chaos that ensued as his partners in crime re-entered the room. We all four watched, momentarily transfixed as he struggled like a child trying to pull off his much younger brother's sweater, all the while wildly waving a loaded long-barreled .38 Smith & Wesson in our presumed direction.

Finally, frustrated but not beaten by the task, he had managed to tear off the egregious garment only to find he had been pointing the weapon menacingly in the direction of his criminal cohorts.

Fighting back the urge to laugh, we were instead forced to accept the gravity of our situation. As they fought amongst themselves, we were left lying prostrate on the pub's beer-soaked carpet, awaiting our fate.

The plan had clearly been to enter the building, threaten the staff, rob the pub of that night's takings and leave. But instead they were now faced with a pair of idiot drunks who knew just enough to stay quiet, but had seen just enough to present a problem. Suddenly and without warning, our man, as if seeing us for the first time, had screamed frustratedly "Why don't I just shoot one of yous?"

This had been met with an uncomfortable silence, broken to all our surprise by my friend extending a finger toward me across the fetid, sodden, ruddy Axminster swirls and uttering in his native Geordie accent, "Shoot him! I've got four kids."

Surprised and angered by this ungenerous northern outburst, they had instead forced us to crawl the length of the pub at gunpoint, bundled us unceremoniously into the men's toilets and ordered us not to move or we would both be shot - kids or no kids.

There fell an awkward and embarrassed silence between us that seemed to last for hours but had likely amounted to little more than minutes. When all of a sudden, for the second time that night, the pub's door had been abruptly kicked open, this time by an armed and balaclavaed SFO squad who were clearly relieved to be late to the party and equally surprised to find us in attendance.

Having freed the brutalised staff, they set about reinstating the 'lock-in' with renewed vigour and enthusiasm. It later came to light that the abortive raid, which had resulted in a barman being stabbed and a friendship sorely tested, had been the result of a petty argument over a rival White City pub darts-match gone wrong.

The next morning a chauffeur-driven limousine had collected me, from my basement flat in Shepherd's Bush and delivered me (still resolutely drunk) to the First Class lounge of a British Airways flight destined for Tokyo.

PERIHELION

PERIHELION

It's London April 1st, 1997, April Fools' Day. Not since the 'Great Comet' of 1811 had the northern hemisphere borne witness to such a celestial show of extravagance. Comet Hale-Bopp arrived suddenly and without fanfare in Notting Hill's night sky and sat there for 569 days. Both the Greeks and Romans had believed comets to be portents of good or ill. I am 39 years old and still a decade away from opening Bankrobber. I am lost and expecting my first child. I had been a jobbing photographer for more than fifteen years during which time I had met John Le Carre's 'Smiley' in the shape of Alec Guinness in a Mayfair Park, arm wrestled with Oliver Reed in a Dorking bar, sat with a nervous Hugh Grant five years before his 'William Thacker' had opened that now famous blue door in the film Notting Hill and had introduced a young Johnny Depp to the piratical rings that would go on to decorate the fingers of his comic character Jack Sparrow. I wasn't lost. I was bored.

As Hale-Bopp had progressed on its perihelion journey across the night sky with its gaseous tail brightening, creating a celestial flare that illuminated the streets below with an eerie argon glow, a fresh fall of snow had settled on the pavement outside Damien Hirst's newly opened Pharmacy restaurant where a line of diners could be seen jockeying for position. But if you had chanced to look up that night beyond and over the rooftops of the neighbouring streets and through the flurries of snow you might have caught sight of a solitary figure darting furtively amid the shadows, leaving in his wake a cunningly appointed trail of profane and political imagery. A prolific and potent series of protestations that were set to influence and shape the next two decades of my life. Hale Bopp had continued on its aphelion path disappearing from our skies as suddenly as it had arrived in December 1999.

MOSSACK FONSECA

MOSSACK FONSECA

There had been a growing sense of anxiety in the air toward the close of 1997. I was fast approaching my fortieth year, Andy Warhol had been dead for some ten years. Hale-Bopp's sudden arrival in the night sky seemed to have exaggerated this sense of unease, its arrival illuminating a train of tragic and catastrophic events. In Northern California, thirty-nine members of the religious cult Heaven's Gate, dressed in matching black tracksuits with Nike trainers, had been persuaded by their leader to drink a lethal cocktail, then told to lie still on their regimented bunks to await the certain transition of their souls to a passing spacecraft flying in the comet's wake. Gianni Versace had been shot dead on the steps of his Miami mansion by the stalker Andrew Cunanan. Princess Diana 'The People's Princess' had been killed in a paparazzi-fuelled car chase. The rich were feeling vulnerable and many had turned to the ownership of art as a panacea, an opiate to sate their growing concerns, a comfort blanket in an increasingly hostile environment.

It was to this ferment on a cold and crisp November evening of the same year that in the packed salesroom of Christie's New York a crowd of more than 2,000 people had gathered, hungry for spectacle and drama. They were there to witness the much anticipated sale of the private collection of Victor and Sally Ganz, dubbed as the 'collectors who never made a mistake' and they had not been disappointed. As the hammer had come down on [Lot no.33] Pablo Picasso's Women of Algiers [Version 0] a new world record had been set, this one lot alone fetching a staggering $31.9m dollars. That such a price had been achieved gave first glimpse of the tip of a sinister disguised iceberg, one cast from the darkly corrupt waters of the Panama Canal, a venal fifty-one mile transactional track, a black strap of stagnant water, bisecting the Isthmus of Panama, joining the Atlantic and Pacific oceans.

It transpired that the Ganz sale was not all what it had purported to be. With the leak of what had later become known as the 'Panama Papers' it was revealed that the collection had been privately purchased for $168m dollars in a secret deal some six months prior to the auction by an offshore shell company registered to the Panamanian law firm Mossack Fonsecca. The intensely private British billionaire currency trader at the centre of the purchase had struck a deal with Christie's that on the same day the purchase was completed the entire collection had been contracted to the auction house with the caveat that it be marketed as the 'Ganz Collection'. So began an elaborate trade that would come to define the 'Art Market' for decades to come, the moment that art had stepped out from the shadows and into the spotlight to claim its place as a global commodity, one that could be traded in parity to both property and stocks but with the clear advantage that there was no regulatory body in place to police or patrol the procurement or disposal of art.

The Ganz's had spent fifty years and $2m dollars, quietly and unassumingly amassing their collection but in the fortnight preceding the sale a record 25,000 visitors had filed through the doors of Christie's New York, an appreciative and democratic audience that had clearly taken comfort from the quiet endeavour of this couple's commitment to their passion. They had succeeded in making Picasso, Jasper Johns, Robert Rauschenberg feel like old friends, the exemplars of their day, who had held our hands through the transition from Expressionism to Abstract Expressionism all now generously displayed under one roof, before being removed, chained and enslaved into the dark and murky world of commerce, destined to become little more than pawns in a complex and manifestly corrupt game.

What had actually happened on that frosty November night, was not as had been assumed a salute to the talent of these giants of the art world. Instead what the packed audience had witnessed that night was a trick, a carefully orchestrated sleight of hand, a 'Three-Card Monte' for grown-ups that in any other context would have had the crowds baying 'cheat'. But never having previously been applied to art, the trick, one heavily veiled and obscured by the polished and respectable veneer of the laudable and much venerated auction house, had drawn only wild applause. The whole elaborate event was a calculated and carefully staged piece of theatre. If the works had failed to exceed their estimate there would have been no loss to the auction house as the works had already been sold. It was the perfect 'short' and with that evening's sale netting a cool $206m dollars, it meant that in just six months the architect of the trick and the complicit auction house had snared a neat $38m dollar reward and as an unintended consequence had lit the blue touchpaper to a new world order.

Meanwhile the old world order had been caught napping. Blindsided by the sudden and uninvited arrival of these arrivistes to the stage, these scurrilously oblique understudies who had been busying themselves in the wings had arrived with a swagger and verve hitherto unseen. The old art world establishment had become lazy and leaden, its bastions watching over an industry serviced by a close-knit clan of young privately schooled gatekeepers practiced at looking down on those outside of their clique. Galleries had in place an unwritten agreement to remain closed on Mondays in a show of civilised contempt to normal working practices. (I had always assumed to allow for the fog of the weekends excesses to clear.) The elite masters of this particular universe had for decades run their businesses from the corridors and private dining rooms of fusty Pall Mall members clubs. Deals had been sealed by handshake. Paperwork had remained studiously sketchy and purposefully imprecise. It was a smug comfortably closed community, dressed in tweed and corduroy and shod with hand-built brogues from Jermyn Street. A uniform broken only by the occasional flourish. A silk cravat or decorative waistcoat to single themselves out from the crowd. Small seditiously subtle signifiers that confirmed and reassured others from within their set.

But no one had warned of the barbarians clamouring at the gates and before it was too late the auction houses, in their blinkered greed, had unwittingly invited the Trojan Horse to within the walls of its citadel and there was no turning back. These young, uninvited interlopers and trespassers, dressed in sharp suits, brandishing their mobile phones, were intent on seizing control of this august institution and making it theirs. To enable this, hastily acquired leases were snapped up at ever more exclusive addresses, bigger, better shinier. An all new playground where they could arrogantly display the spoils of their plunder, vast glazed walls were erected from behind which they could parade their wares like so many puffed up peacocks, boastfully rattling their iridescent eyes at bedazzled and awed onlookers. The City-learnt tricks of their past trading careers had set them in good stead for this new adventure, one that was to be a mercilessly and cynically applied Ponzi scheme that would fuel two decades of greed, excess and reckless speculation.

In May 2015 Pablo Picasso's 'Women of Algiers (Version 0)' came back to auction at Christie's New York fetching $206m dollars.

Y2K

Y2K

Malibu California 2000. As dawn had broken over the Pacific Ocean on that, the first day of a new century, the hysterical predictions and growing disquiet, that a programming oversight known as the Millennium Bug but more sinisterly named 'Y2K' was set to wreak global havoc on the turning of the century, bringing computer systems to their knees, planes to fall from the sky and random nuclear launches to occur, but the much anticipated and feared trauma had come to nothing.

The previous day in something akin to the 'Last Supper' I had eaten and drank my way through a twenty course dinner to see in the new century, a bacchanalian feast served over eight hours, laid out on an expansive table on the foreshore of a lavishly-appointed, rented house, with views across the Malibu Bay, an apocalyptic apéritif designed to quell the nerves of the gathered apostles, whose palpable sense of panic on the approach of midnight only partially obscured by the abandon of gluttony.

To me it felt like we had been gorging senselessly on the excesses of the past six years, the 'Dot-com boom' had seemed unstoppable. Tech stocks and shares were flipped for fun, start-ups and so-called incubators were traded like sweets at a rabid pick-n-mix party. The advent and advances of the internet had enabled everyone to be a speculator, like the Klondike gold rush a century earlier. There had been an electronic stampede of these latter-day prospectors, their sieves and spades replaced by cell phones and laptops. Rich seams from the Silicon Valley basin, were been weighed and traded with slavish disregard toward any tangible value. But on this fine and first morning of the new century as I had looked out across the ocean, surrounded by the trappings of wealth and success, something felt wrong. I had indeed attended the party and had borne witness to the extravagant pyrotechnics that had bade farewell to the old and ushered in the new. But as so often before, I had felt distant and disconnected.

A heretic, a Judas, who had never really been a true believer at the altar of avarice, never been persuaded by the valley's enthusiastic preachers with their messianic machinations on Mammon.

I had remained firmly and stubbornly outside of their church, looking in. An agnostic interloper who was once again lost, bored or worse… both.

Five years earlier in a small back room in San Jose, Northern California, a young software engineer and his small team were putting the finishing touches to a groundbreaking e-commerce website, a consumer-to-consumer platform that would later become known as eBay. A radical game-changer that would transform the way the world would buy and sell art.

Four years on, and on the other side of the Atlantic, in a similarly small back-room in West London's Notting Hill, I was busy putting into play my own considerably less ambitious plan but one that would nonetheless directly benefit from the endeavours of that team of maverick Californian outliers. Their efforts were to enable a serendipitous chain of events that would create a new wave of young collectors and dealers.

A wave I was unwittingly well-placed to ride.

But it would take the cataclysmic events of September the eleventh, 2001 to divert me from my previously planned career trajectory and to unexpectedly write me into this new story.

Lying on a hospital bed in Dorchester general hospital with a shattered spiral fracture to the base of my left tibia, heavily sedated and wretchedly hungover, I was watching the repeated screening of what appeared to be a disaster movie featuring a commercial airline slicing casually through the third tier of the second tower of New York's World Trade Center. Without the benefit of sound I had found the bizarre metronomic repetition strangely calming. But during the coming hours as I had gradually sobered and the morphine fog had begun to lift, I realised that what I had been watching was, far from a clumsy scheduling error screened on the wing of a provincial accident and emergency ward, but instead, the tragic unfolding of a callous attack to the very heart of western capitalism.

The twin towers that my twenty-seven-year-old self, had once stared up at in awe lay collapsed in a catastrophic crescendo of concrete and dust and demolished dreams. Everything had changed.

MY DADDY WAS A BANKROBBER

MY DADDY WAS A BANKROBBER

Freshly emboldened by the successful sale of Banksy's 'WHAT?' and keen to benefit from the growing press speculation that Bankrobber, rather than being merely an arbitrary seller of a now controversial artwork, might in some way be linked to the elusive artist. Rumour and innuendo had abounded and questions asked, was it really a coincidence that this humble little space should have sprung up on a largely ignored backwater, tucked away behind Notting Hill's achingly cool Westbourne Grove, a street that bordered the northernmost aspect of Banksy's playground, with Ladbroke Grove to its west and Portobello Road to its east? A Bermuda Triangle of activity that (since the late nineties) had become the artist's chosen canvas, hitting railway bridges, private residences, curb stones and clubs, a neighbourhood now widely recognised as being the artist's West London stage and it was onto this stage that I had stepped in the spring of 2007.

To my surprise I had begun to rather enjoy the attention that this unexpected speculation was bringing. People were actively trying to join the dots between Banksy and Bankrobber and it was within this ferment that 'A Tale of Two Robins' had begun in earnest.

Far from pouring cold water on these inferred assertions I had actively encouraged them. Initially I had satisfied myself that this had been a partisan act, shrewd business practice rather than any sign of an increasingly out of control alter ego. But in my darker moments I was beginning to have my doubts. The more I denied being involved with the artist, the more convinced people became that I was holding out on them. More intriguingly there was even a faction within the press who had entertained the notion that I might in fact be Banksy.

Logically the successful sale of 'WHAT?' should have been the end of a colourful adventure and that when the work had left, like Elvis exiting the building, a calm should have descended. But I had tasted success and what had been conceived as a small scale venture, a local art gallery and framers with modest ambition, now held little interest for me and for the first time since stepping out of that limousine on that December day some twenty years earlier, I had felt elated and alive. The ego had landed, and like a cuckoo in the nest it was famished and greedy for more.

It's December 1st, 2007, I am 47 years old and walking through security at John F. Kennedy International airport. It is the second time that the now PR mogul Matthew Freud has unwittingly enabled me the luxury of flight. But I was here on a very different mission than that of my previous sojourn. This was to be a four-day 'get rich quick scheme'. Far from allowing the adrenalin rush of the 'WHAT?' sale to dissipate, I had instead hatched an audacious and ambitious plan to nurture and grow the seed of a myth by taking temporary possession of a small NYC Chelsea townhouse situated over four floors. In partnership with a piratical book trader and a flagrantly artificial art dealer we were bringing Banksy to New York. It was to take the form of a five-day residency under the purposefully vague 'Banksy NYC' banner. We would be hosting a thinly veiled show that implied authenticity whilst in fact being little more than an avaricious attempt on our part to sell a hastily cobbled together collection of secondary market works. The kernel of doubt as to the ethics of this project that had haunted me in the days prior to arriving had all but evaporated on seeing a corrugated steel wall festooned with our posters, featuring Banksy's cheekily appropriated 'Monkey Queen'. Dozens of tiara-wearing chimps had stared out at me from the gloom, each set against a colour-drained Union Jack with the word B A N K S Y underscored by NYC 2007. Every available surface between West 38th and West

27th had been covered by this fly-posted simian salute to its newly adopted prodigal son. If it looked like a Banksy show then to an unwitting New York audience it would be a Banksy show. And in any case the genie was out of the bottle and I was determined it wasn't going back anytime soon and with the growing realisation that the very thing that made Banksy unique, his much lauded anonymity, was precisely what made him vulnerable to our plan.

Come the morning of the opening and in a damaged haze of alcohol-fuelled chaos we had transformed the quirky but beautifully appointed townhouse The Vanina Holasek Gallery into a largely blacked-out manifestation of what we believed a Banksy show might look like. Daubing the walls in faux (and largely vacuous) misleading instructions, we had installed a rented NYC crossing light, which had flashed 'Walk - Don't Walk' as if imbued with some darker instruction or intuition.

I don't recall a great deal from that first day other than on leaving a nearby bar, which we had made our base camp (one regularly frequented by the British actors Tim Roth and Gary Oldman, the first of which in a different life I had briefly shared an East End address and unaccountably been mistaken for on more than one occasion since). A beautiful fresh blanket of snow had begun to form and to my surprise, on turning onto Chelsea's West 27th Street, I'd been met by the sight of a long three-deep line of people snaking around the block, patiently huddled against the falling snow. I had taken a moment to consider how they might react to the entirely fraudulent manifestation of our making. Then shaking off my doubt I had arrogantly stridden to the front of the line and with a theatrical flourish had assumed my newly rehearsed role.

For four days straight the line continued as hundreds of adoring fans made the journey to our little folly on Chelsea's West 27th street. The atmosphere within had been one of almost reverential awe as they had traipsed the four floors in hushed silence as if visiting a place of worship. The whispered comments and respectful atonement that the works had instilled belied all our expectations. But as the week progressed, it dawned on us that far from being the promised financial success we had hoped for, we had instead created a shrine to the very artist whose endeavours we had hoped to plunder. Perhaps on reflection we should have looked to the scriptures before embarking on this particularly inept escapade. We had bought avarice to the temple and we had been duly punished.

And Jesus went into the temple of God, and cast out all them that sold and bought in the temple, and overthrew the tables of the money changers, and the seats of them that sold doves, And said unto them, It is written, My house shall be called the house of prayer; but ye have made it a den of thieves.

And so it was that on the sixth day of December, this particular den of thieves had packed up shop without having sold a single artwork. Ironically had we simply charged a $5 dollar admission fee we would have made the very fortune we had sought. Dispirited but not down, we did that uniquely British thing in the face of failure and proceeded to get fabulously drunk. The party queen of Manhattan Amy Sacco had generously opened the doors to her exclusive 'Bungalow 8' night club for our wrap party. Opened in late 2002 on West 27th and 10th, it was the 'go-to' celebrity hang-out, replete with palm trees and poolside murals, although for all I can remember it might as well have been a sandpit in a cellar. But it was much later, on the twelfth-floor of the Gansevoort Hotel in the city's newly fashionable Meatpacking district that I had chosen to party. The whole floor had been secured as a playground for some minor British royal and their friends to host a pre 'Art Miami' soiree. The elegant Rastafarian doorman looked on doubtfully as I weaved my way unsteadily toward the elevator but my new friend had pre-arranged my security clearance and on exiting the elevator at the twelfth floor, I was reluctantly ushered along a corridor by an armed personal protection officer to my destination, whereupon the door to Room 1203 was enthusiastically thrown open to the hypnotic strains of Nouvelle Vague's 2004 cover of Jello Biafra's 'Too Drunk To Fuck'.

It would be another six years before Banksy took his hugely successful month-long residency to New York.

GYPSIES TRAMPS AND THIEVES

GYPSIES TRAMPS AND THIEVES

Robin mate, Luke says, the gypsies have just tried to sell Peter a gun for fuck sakes!!

So had come the call from the clearly bewildered and angry personal manager of the errant and erstwhile lover and libertine Peter Doherty, who, now permanently banished from the North London home of supermodel and cultural icon Kate Moss following the collapse of their tempestuous on-off relationship, was currently residing (at my behest) in a broken-down trailer on the outskirts of a traveller community nestled in the shadow of the Westway, the raised concrete highway which strode purposefully out of Edgware, heading out west over Paddington, Bayswater and Notting Hill then landing with some authority in White City before dispersing chaotically to the outer edges of West London. This disparate enclave formed of a triangle of neglected wasteland, somehow overlooked during the slum clearances of the late 1960s, was watched over by the ever vigilant eye of Luke the 'Metal Man', a vast individual who's appearance suggested he bathed exclusively in used engine oil that had rendered him an alarming metallic, steely blue hue. Indeed only the palms of his hands hinted at any possible ethnicity, drenched as they were in a perennial layer of Swarfega, a dark green thixotropic substance used to cut through oil and grease. His fiefdom which he guarded with an almost military zeal was littered with a baffling assortment of objét-trouvé [junk] whose only commonality were they were all fashioned out of metal, thus provoking his moniker. His formidable countenance was matched only by that of his dog, a truly fearsome looking creature, standing in excess of ten hands in height and sharing the same deathly pall of his master. This West London Cerberus had ensured that even the most foolhardy paparazzi would hesitate to pry. In truth the only real threat this canine colossus presented was that brushing up against him would likely leave you feeling like a victim of the catastrophic Torrey Canyon oil spill.

Four weeks earlier and I am sat in the luxurious confines of my newly adopted office, the red velvet-lined booth, of next-door's Lonsdale Club. Surrounded by the customary towers of boxes and crates of wine and beer stacked high all about me, I am locked in deep discussion with the redoubtable and charismatic Andy Boyd, the personal manager of the former frontman of Indie Rock band 'The Libertines'. He was busy explaining that, "He likes to be called Peter, not Pete, and its Doherty not Docherty".

It is the spring of 2007 and having been recently released from a short stay at Her Majesty's pleasure at HM Wormwood Scrubs, just a stone's throw from his precious Loftus Road, Peter was eagerly preparing the ground for a comeback, having recently formed breakaway band 'Babyshambles'.

He was now working on the final edit of his soon to be published diaries 'The Books of Albion'. His manager had gone on to explain that Peter had for some time been creating paintings using his own blood and that he felt Bankrobber had the requisite reputation to act as the perfect launch pad for his client's artistic output. In exchange for displaying these works of challenging content and questionable ability Bankrobber would be given the exclusive opportunity to host Peter's much anticipated book launch.

Still smarting from the failure of the recent Banksy New York debacle, I had considered this a much needed distraction and moreover with his star seemingly firmly in the ascendance and his relationship with Kate Moss guaranteeing column inches at his every travail, it might just provide a way out of the current Banksy impasse. Above all else, it sounded like it could be fun, a holiday away from the daily grind of 'Bankrobber-bashing' that had seemed to fill my days since my return to London. And after all... where could be the harm in it.

Peter had entered the room suddenly and without warning, his trademark trilby hat framing a quizzical pallid expression for all the world as if he had happened upen this bloody display quite by chance. In spite of his famously chaotic lifestyle and somewhat archaic and shambolic dress sense, he carried himself with remarkable grace and poise within the tight confines of Bankrobber's cramped space and I had been struck by the sheer scale of him, not the pin thin poet I had imagined but a tall robust figure who moved balletically and purposefully across the room. But it had been his voice that had so disarmed me. In an imperceptibly soft and polite tone he had asked if I had a canvas that he could have.

I had been supplying his manager with a steady flow of canvases since our first meeting in the misplaced hope of influencing their outcome. Now with Peter stood in front of me, my opportunity arrived. I had been struck dumb, left only to watch on in silence as he had grappled with the largest of the available canvases, finally putting it to rest on a large central table before theatrically pulling out a blood-filled syringe from a concealed poacher's pocket deep within the lining of his elaborately adorned greatcoat and proceeded to sketch out his now familiar self-portrait, then signing it with a flourish before stabbing the needle dramatically into the eye of the full stop, hesitating only momentarily to wonder at his own work, before turning on his heels and leaving as suddenly as he had arrived.

The crimson silhouette left glistening on the primed white surface in the failing afternoon light, the abandoned syringe standing sentry straight against the canvas as a blacked out BMW had sped west along Lonsdale Road stopping just long enough for Peter to fall gracefully into the back seat, then he was gone. The three German students who had been animatedly discussing the show's content had fallen silent on his arrival and had stood statue still throughout the performance, an audience of three to an intimate and unique piece of theatre. Their faces drained of blood, they had trailed wordlessly out of the gallery in awed silence. Had Peter rehearsed his role, he could not have performed it more proficiently and professionally. The painting titled 'Needle' went on to feature as the centrepiece of 'Bloodworks', Peter's controversial exhibition of fourteen previously unseen works.

"The controversial 'Babyshambles' frontman set to make £500,000 from the sale of 14 paintings and several prints when his bloodworks exhibition opens at Notting Hill's Bankrobber gallery on Tuesday May 15th."

So had read the headlines, not just in the London papers but across the Globe. Quite unintentionally, it seemed I had put a flame to the blue touchpaper of a skyrocket that had set the world talking. The news of the imminent opening had caused an outpouring of rage and disgust. Not only had this libertine and lothario defiled and derailed the career of Croydon's most celebrated daughter but he now had the temerity to masquerade as an artist in its purest guise. Journalists and filmmakers had clamoured to be part of the story. Each day leading up to the launch, I had been asked to comment on Peter's practice and purpose.

Robin Barton, of the Bankrobber gallery, presenting the show, claimed the medium was very appropriate for Doherty. "His use of blood lends itself perfectly to exploring the extraordinary personal and physical intensity that characterises so much of Peter's life and work as an artist in the broadest sense." This deeply disingenuous diatribe had been met with unbridled enthusiasm and glee from interviewers from across several continents. Japan, Italy, Germany, Netherlands and Russia were just a few of those who had paid lip-service to this preposterous and pompous assertion. But the British press were having none of it. They had smelt blood quite literally and were out to scupper the venture at any cost.

Medical experts were called upon to pass judgement as to the moral and ethical implications of displaying these works. It had even been suggested that they might present a health hazard to the visiting public if the show was allowed to go ahead. The same esteemed BBC art critic that would go on to maul and malign my efforts to sell Banksy's 'Slave Labour' some five years into the future, had entered the fray casting a disparaging eye over the works and proclaiming them with some disdain as, "having no artistic merit whatsoever", but despite this vicious and unprovoked attack, the public's appetite had remained undaunted. So what if this was a flagrant case of The Emperor's New Clothes! His public hadn't cared, they adored their monarch and had remained true. This paired with Kate's unquenchable kudos, had far outweighed any consideration and concern from a crusty and constipated member of the cognoscente.

The crescendo of criticism had continued to grow as the opening date had approached but my focus had been on the more pressing issue as to whether his mercurial manager could match his promise to deliver Peter to the all-important book signing arranged to mark and celebrate the launch of his soon to be published diaries. This hope had been dealt a double blow on hearing the news that a new date for a hearing for charges of possession was to be brought forward. But even more troubling was the news that he had simply forgotten to attend his own publisher's dinner held in his honour much to the chagrin of its grandees who despite the barely decipherable prose, had put great store on the much anticipated journals. I hadn't known it at the time but the star's seemingly unstoppable ascendance was much like the freshly lit skyrocket - about to explode dramatically, its embers extinguished by the night sky, leaving only a memory of what might have been.

Peter did get his day in court and I in turn, had my day in the limelight. Good to his word, Andy Boyd had delivered the seemingly undeliverable and Peter to his credit had played his part with charm in abundance, arriving in the same blacked out BMW that had whisked him away just weeks earlier. He had stepped theatrically out onto the stage that was Bankrobber and with a low sweeping bow to the waiting paparazzi, had proceeded to take his place at the club's top table ready to receive a seemingly endless line of adoring fans. I had been taken by his innate ability to make each and every one of them feel they were the sole focus of his attention, his democracy was limitless, children, dogs, cleaners, concierge and clerics were all received with the same intimate charm.

Prior to his anticipated arrival, the Lonsdale club's security had arranged to have the road closed at each end to ramp up the excitement. Local radio provided live updates. Reports talked of sightings of Peter being seen on his way to the 'Hotel in the Sky', his Hackney hideaway. Others of him being spotted on his way out of London toward Kate's Cotswolds home.

It was only looking back that I realised how different things might have been. If like so many times before Peter had chosen another path on that spring afternoon. But he hadn't and fortune had smiled on me. Only when the line of enthusiastic acolytes had finally subsided and the club's doors pulled shut, was I able to relax and bask in the glory of the afternoon's event. With the book signing now a 'fait accompli' we had set about enjoying the moment, laughing and sharing stories of hedonistic excess. Much of the rest of that night remains a blur, one obscured by the generous application of alcohol and adrenalin. The velvet-lined booth cocooning us from the growing hoards who had descended on the club in the hope of catching sight of their favourite libertine and his entourage. Like the scene from 'The Godfather' whispered introductions were made and protocols observed. Throughout Peter had played his role with an almost childlike enthusiasm, all the while his phone pressed firmly to one ear in whispered conversation. He was both in the room and elsewhere, occasionally pushing some food about the lavishly catered table before settling greedily on a crème brûlée then returning to his hushed negotiations.

As the night had progressed, rumours had spread that Kate might be joining us, I had considered that after all it might indeed have been she that Peter had been locked in conversation with throughout the evening but what neither I, nor those around the table that night knew, was that the party was all but over for Peter. Leaving the club much later he had taken the opportunity to grab the antique Union Jack from Bankrobber, draping it over his shoulders for the benefit of the remaining paparazzi, defiant and drunk, an emperor swathed in the fineries of his beloved Albion.

But it had been an ill wind that had blown in to fill the void of the couple's turbulent relationship and the maelstrom of death that had swirled around Peter in the months that followed seemed to eclipse and obscure his promised potential.

In the end it hadn't been the truly troubling thought of Peter Doherty being sold a gun that had resulted in him being prised from the reluctant oily grip of West London's 'Metal Man'. Rather, it was a probation order that uniquely forbade him from having a London postcode. It was this, no doubt well intentioned, instruction that had provoked the move to 'Sturmy House' a nine-bedroomed red brick mansion owned by the Earl of Cardigan, located in the depths of Wiltshire, a move that had been a purposeful attempt to put some distance between Peter and the paparazzi, whom he had considered to blame for the ultimate collapse of his relationship with Kate Moss.

It had been shortly after his triumphant book launch that the pair had finally parted ways for good and although it would be an exaggeration to suggest that the event had in any way hastened the inevitable, her absence had certainly been noted in the press and on reflection the hushed telephone reveries that had so absorbed him throughout that evening might indeed have pointed to him having been involved in more of his amorous adventuring. But who was I to know or judge? What had become clear is that now Kate had been rescued from the clutches of this troubled troubadour his currency had dropped significantly and by the time I had reached 'Sturmy House' some months later, it was apparent that things were not going well.

I had been persuaded to visit on the news that Peter had been busy painting away prolifically on the regularly proffered canvases. The exterior of his country retreat was unremarkable but for a broken-down dress mannequin holding forth a tatty Union Jack flag, and the ground floor windows appeared to have been painted out (presumably to deter prying eyes) but on entering the property on that cold autumn afternoon I had been struck by the sheer bleakness of its interior. Barely any furniture was in evidence and any light that had penetrated the crudely painted-out windows had presented as a gloomy kaleidoscopic mess. Those surfaces that did exist were littered with half empty bottles, the wreckage of takeaway cartons and dozens of empty cigarette packets. Discarded needles were strewn everywhere and many of the walls were daubed with clumsy unintelligible scrawl, bizarrely punctuated with the random markings of cats' paws that in some rooms extended to the ceilings. I had been hoping for a modern day Charleston House but had instead been presented by something that more resembled an anteroom to Dante's Underworld. The two young girls who had greeted us on arrival explained that Peter was asleep and they had been instructed he mustn't be disturbed. Ushered silently through to Peter's 'Painting Studio', I had been pained to find dozens of my donated canvases in various states of dereliction, propped up against the walls, their primed surfaces scarred by the same scant representations of nothing much at all. I had considered that if all these random markings put together with those from the walls of the previous rooms,could be condensed and applied to just a single canvas there might be at best the makings of a painting, albeit in the very loosest sense of the word.

Sensing my disappointment, his magnanimous manager had gone on to explain that they were very much works in progress. Not wanting to have had a wasted journey (and taking pity on the two waifs tasked with entertaining us) we took off in search of a pub where we might wait for news of Peter's awakening.

Entering the 'Robin Hood Inn' at Durley that afternoon was every bit the village cliché. The theatrically creaky door opening onto an audience of local drinkers who had eyed us with near comical contempt and surly suspicion. Settling at a corner table, we watched on in bewildered silence as our two companions devoured their way greedily through two vast plates stacked-high with food. Clearly the catering at 'Stormy House', as it had been re-christened, left something to be desired and it was apparent that this pair of famished would-be ingénues had discovered that fame could be a hungry game. Meanwhile back at the house, there had been stirrings from upstairs. The news was that Peter was hungry. The girls, sated to the point of narcolepsy had searched in vain for a solution, finally singling out a solitary potato from the darkest depths of the otherwise empty cupboards, the discovery of which had presented them with a culinary conundrum as clearly neither had any concept of how, or indeed if, this meagre offering might be presented as a meal. On leaving later that afternoon I had looked back to see the pair still starring pensively and plaintively at the single tuber.

Peter never did appear on that afternoon or on any other since, and the paintings owed, remain a distant and unfulfilled promise.

It had been more than a dozen years since. When idly rummaging through the maze of fairground paraphernalia and neon signage of Margate's 'Fort Road Yard', a treasure trove for the prop and theatre crowd that flocked down from London at the weekends to visit this coastal cornucopia in the hope of finding the un-findable, that I had caught sound of that unique voice, the imperceptibly soft tone that immediately transported me back to that May afternoon all those years earlier. The unmistakable voice belonging to that of one Peter Doherty, painter, poet and performer. I had looked up sharply, in time to catch sight of him descending a rickety step ladder from a corrugated steel eerie set high in the gods of this cavernous emporium, a place surrounded by disenfranchised and ornately painted 'Fairground Gallopers' long since cut tether from their carousels. Jugglers' batons littered the floor below, trapeze swings fell motionless from the building's vaulted ceilings and cracked-out clowns lay slumped on grubby cream vinyl covered couches in sinister slumber. Standing resplendent in a stained sand coloured suit in the argon glow of the neon, he had looked every bit the master of this his very own circus of the absurd.

Months later the town's local newspaper had announced that the Babyshambles frontman along with his Libertine friends were to open a seven-bedroom hotel to be named 'The Albion Rooms' that promised views across the Thanet coastline and would include a bar called 'The Waste Land' named in homage to the poet T.S. Elliot who had penned the poem just two doors down from this fitting new chapter in the artists life.

"It might be a while before we challenge the Savoy or the Grand Budapest in the hotel stakes, but we've put a lot of love into this. Meanwhile it's a colourful and inspiring home for the Libertines and I look forward to the Albion Rooms being our very own Warholian Factory,"

Carl Barât of the Libertines.

'Sequel to the Prequel' was the third and last studio album to be recorded by Babyshambles before they disbanded under a cloud of 'artistic differences'. In a synchronicitous twist of fate, its cover artwork was provided by the artist Damien Hirst.

PRICK

PRICK

It is a beautiful spring morning in March 2008, three young strangers are sat in a row with their backs to the street, their spokesperson earnestly explaining the detail of their acquisition of a Banksy artwork, salvaged from a builder's skip in Liverpool. Explaining that they believed it formed part of the artist's contribution to Liverpool's 2004 Arts Biennial, it featured a bored and bespectacled gallery official sat slumped lazily beside a blank wall on which was spray-painted an ornate golden picture frame, within which the word 'Prick' had been angrily applied.

This meeting, like so many since the widely publicised sale of 'WHAT?', had become something of a ritual. Each Saturday morning, on raising Bankrobber's steel shutters, I would repeat-play Bob Dylan's Hurricane and wait. "While Rubin sits like Buddha in a ten-foot cell, an innocent man in a living hell' is precisely how I was beginning to feel. Like a Catholic priest at his confessional, I would sit and listen to preposterous tales of missed opportunities, drunkenly stumbled upon road signs that their newly adopted owners felt were their ticket out of poverty. A tawdry queue of liars, cheats and chancers. But these three were refreshingly clean, calm and lucid. Their story made sense and was evidentially convincing. The only problem was that they had already approached another party, an established Mayfair gallery that had promised them a guaranteed six-figure sum but in return had demanded exclusivity. This knowledge had jolted me out of the belief that I was the appointed one, the proprietor of a unique one-stop shop for all things authentically Banksy. More crushingly the owner of the august and esteemed Mayfair establishment was a grown up and very much part of the art establishment, one that would surely close ranks against an outsider and most particularly one from the wrong side of Park Lane.

I had lost 'PRICK' to a greater and more determined force than my own and as a result was plummeted into a fog of self-doubt and depression.

Twenty years earlier on an unremarkable January evening and I'm visiting the artist Damien Hirst's recently opened 'Pharmacy' restaurant. Created on the site of 'Cleopatra's Taverna', with its tired facade featuring a huge, incongruous mural of crudely painted 'Shahrazad dancers', a Notting Hill institution that for as long as anyone could remember had offered nightly Greek dancing that had incorporated boisterous and rowdy plate smashing as part of the dining experience, a now unimaginable health and safety hiatus. In sharp contrast 'Pharmacy' with its knowing manner and sleek lines was a cold blooded and arrogant reinterpretation of the space. From its inception it had courted controversy, stymieing a failed attempt to block the use of the word 'Pharmacy' by the Royal Pharmaceutical Society who had claimed that it might be mistaken as an actual dispensary – ironically, not an entirely inaccurate assertion if you included the nightly activities and proclivities indulged by its elite patrons. The fiercely vying egos of the newly anointed king of the YBA movement, pitched against the formidable influence of my unwitting patron Matthew Freud and the fiery genius of Marco Pierre White had ensured it was an instant success with the fast and fashionable. But almost as quickly, as was typical of this fickle set, it had fallen out of fashion, instead becoming the new go-to venue for the aspirational bridge and tunnel set that travelled in from Essex and beyond, attracted and informed by the release of Richard Curtis's horribly prescriptive hit movie 'Notting Hill', an anodised, ethnically cleansed vision of creative harmony and hope.

The restaurant's after-parties however had become the thing of legend. The press regularly reported rumours of dark drug-fuelled excess and I was anxious to be a part of it. Access to these esteemed soirees was by no means a given. However on a number of occasions in those early weeks, most usually after a long and languorous lunch at the discreetly bohemian Julie's Bar, followed by a visit to the fabulously louche 192 Wine Bar (marshalled by Freddie, it's magnificently elegant maître d') then further buoyed by a misplaced need for additional 'refreshment', I would find myself pushing arrogantly past the eager line of patient diners and being ushered upstairs into the restaurant's inner sanctum. There the Allen brothers, Keith and Kevin, could be found holding court alongside the Clash's Paul Simonon, Kate Moss and of course at its epicentre sat astride his throne, the purveyor and curator of all that lay before him, Damien Hirst.

I had been on the fringes of the area's party circuit long enough to know how to play it. As I had sat, surrounded by the great and the good, I had wondered at the preposterous ostentation of it all, its bloated arrogance had momentarily sobered me. It had been seven years since I had stood in front of the artists elegiac 'The Physical Impossibility of Death in the Mind of Someone Living' a two meter long Tiger Shark suspended poetically in a tank of formaldehyde. Back then I had been inexplicably moved and immediately convinced that I was staring into the eyes of a creature made immortal by the work of a genius. But now as I sat in that same artist's grotesquely gaudy parody palace with its faux medicine cabinets and pill-littered wallpaper, I had felt cheated, the sombre religiosity of the artist's early works having been replaced by a conceited scornful neglectfulness, a slothful and lazy example of vanitas. And as I had sat, ever more intoxicated, I imagined myself like Jonah in the belly of the whale, surrounded by the seething bloated baubles of greed and excess. I had come to this modern day Nineveh and I did not like what I had seen.

But in the end, it was neither God nor Mammon that had bought this particular citadel to heel. Rather it was the restaurant critics, vengeful at their exclusion from the elite parties, who had instituted 'a night of the long knives' and had railed against the restaurant owners and their apparent indifference toward their diners' plight. Excoriating reviews along with mocking and cruel characterisations of its denizens had resulted in a dwindling and increasingly unenthusiastic crowd. The parties thinned and diluted and when finally its emperor decamped to the more rarified air of Soho's Colony Rooms and its neighbouring Groucho Club, what had remained resembled little more than a ransacked altar to self-aggrandisement, a narcissistic and empty conceit.

It is October 19th, 2004, almost a year to the day that Hirst's Pharmacy restaurant had quietly and without due notice closed its doors for the last time, leaving behind only the ghosts of excess to stagger aimlessly amid the isles of the soon-to-be-opened Marks & Spencer food hall. In stark contrast Sotheby's sale room had paid host to a crowd of more than a thousand, its number swelled by dealers, collectors and small-time souvenir hunters all hungry to own part of, or bear witness to, a bizarre clearance sale of the fixtures and fittings of an institution that had, albeit briefly, served as a flagship to Tony Blair's Cool Britannia. As the final hammer fell that evening an astonishing £11.1 million had been secured, making Hirst Britain's wealthiest living artist, the sale acting as an uncanny precursor to his next Sotheby's adventure just four years later, Beautiful Inside My Head Forever, that was to net the artist a sinisterly synergetic £111million.

As darkness fell on that first night over Hirst's empty and failed Notting Hill venture, two-hundred miles away on Liverpool's Lime Street, sandwiched between a tanning salon and run-down Irish bar, a shadowy figure was spraying the final flourish to a hastily stencilled mural. A bleeding, blue full stop punctuating the single but succinct word PRICK. Bankrobber took back possession of the Liverpool mural after the Mayfair gallery had failed to convince its esteemed patrons as to the value and efficacy of a crudely stenciled portrayal of a slovenly gallery attendant, guarding a seemingly empty gesture.

[PRICK] Stencil & Spray Paint on marine ply - Sold £225,000

DO YOU KNOW WHO I AM

DO YOU KNOW WHO I AM

It is early January 2008 and as the steel curtain came down on another Saturday at Bankrobber, the phone rang out and I had reluctantly picked it up. A hostile woman's voice snapped at me "Do you know who I am?". This would be the first of many such calls over the coming weeks, which would mark a very different landscape than that of the previous year.

The initial celebratory swagger that had followed the headline-stealing sale of 'What?' had been replaced by a growing sense of unease. The wildly misjudged antics of that same year's fatally flawed New York debacle had left me feeling paranoid, unsettled and near broke. We had flown too close to the sun and we had been duly punished, but in our absence the press had enjoyed their own party. The London Evening Standard had run a front page reporting the 'What?' sale as having netted Bankrobber a cool half a million pounds.

It was an exaggerated and unfounded boast but one that had triggered unwarranted interest from some dubious parties. The accusations of theft and double-dealing had abounded in the weeks following the work's sale and dark disturbing rumours had begun to circulate, the most alarming pointing to a not entirely implausible link between Banksy's recently appointed manager and a notorious West London crime family.

This news had darkened my mood considerably and over the following months the boredom of those Saturday morning soliloquies, had been replaced by an uneasy sense of paranoia. The

Pandora's box of intrigue, energy and excitement that had defined the Bankrobber of only six months earlier had been replaced with a creeping sense of dread. It seemed the space had turned its back on me, or I on it, either way the magic was gone and I had employed every and any excuse to stay away.

By March of that same year it was apparent that the honeymoon period was over for Bankrobber. The excitement and energy that had followed its opening had rapidly been replaced by hostile suspicion. Cyber-warriors busied themselves in their bedsits, penning personal attacks and criticisms against both it and myself. Bankrobber rapidly became the target of scorn and anger. The driving narrative being that Banksy was a Robin Hood for our times, a charmed Artful Dodger, a subversive and celebrated hero of the people. I, on the other hand, as the architect and driving force behind Bankrobber, had been portrayed as an evil and self-serving pariah, hell-bent on making profit from the artist's munificent largesse, in short, a bounder and a blaggard. A bad lot.

I considered the only reasonable response to this growing criticism would be to put on a show of defiance. My chosen weapon of retaliation was to install a controversially acquired six meter Banksy mural featuring nine and a half crudely stenciled chimpanzees, wearing placards with the slogan 'Laugh Now But One Day We'll be in Charge'. This monumental work, originally sited behind a bar in a Brighton nightclub, had filled the walls of Bankrobber, spelling out a clear message of confrontational disobedience to all the doubters and haters that might come by. I then quietly retreated to my newly adopted headquarters located in the deep and dark recesses of the 'Lonsdale Club' next door. With its sumptuous red velvet-lined booths and its nighttime vibe, it provided the perfect sanctuary from where to consider my next play.

This new dynamic calmed my nerves considerably, bringing with it the additional advantage of a further layer of security in the shape of its enigmatic doorman Damian, a well-connected and charismatic foot soldier to the very same crime family, whose veiled threats had signalled my retreat. The phone had continued to ring throughout that spring but I had resolved to remain conspicuous by my absence. Sitting calmly amid the chaotic daily deliveries of liquor and laundry, I had felt for the first time in a very long time both vindicated and valid, paranoia replaced by a newly realised sense of purpose. If Banksy was to be lauded as this Robin Hood character, then I would present myself as his self-appointed nemesis, his Baird of Bristol pitched against my Sheriff of [Nottingham] Notting Hill Gate.

The Addams Family was a popular 1960's fictional, American black comedy which ran for thirteen years, it featured a macabre family headed by Gomez and Morticia Addams, that included a giant doorman named Lurch and a disembodied hand called Thing. It ran for 64 episodes, the last being screened in October 1977.

Their [pseudo-Latin] family credo ran as "Sic gorgiamus allos subjectatos - *We gladly feast on those who would subdue us*".

PEST CONTROL

PEST CONTROL

Pest Control is a handling service acting on behalf of the artist Banksy. We answer enquiries and determine whether he was responsible for making a certain piece of artwork and issue paperwork if this is the case. ... Banksy is not represented by any other gallery or institution - So had read the endorsement applied to www.pestcontroloffice.com

Freed from the shackles of my cell, emboldened by my new surroundings and with the Chimps now permanently in residence as Bankrobber's appointed guardians, I felt able to consider how to manage the very real threat that Pest Control's creation had represented to the success of my endeavours. Ostensibly set up to weed out fakes and forgeries, it soon became apparent that its real purpose was to stymie any and all attempts to sell, market or manage the artist's Street Works.

The most significant damage to creating a market for these marginalised works was that, from the outset, all the major auction houses had fallen in step and accepted the artist's edict that street pieces or works deemed by the artist not to have been created for resale would not be admitted into any reputable auction sale. In return, Pest Control (at the behest of their commander and chief) had created a certification process that would support and facilitate a secondary market for the artist's works. This shrewd move on the artist's part had an immediate and profound impact on my business. My get-rich-quick scheme had hit the rails before it even had a chance to gather steam, a move that overnight had rendered the artist's street works valueless albeit not entirely worthless. I had been outmanoeuvred and it had looked disastrously akin to Checkmate.

For some time I had wrestled to find a solution to this apparent impasse. But before resigning and surrendering my King, I had determined to make one last move in an attempt to parry the attack. It had been after another long day at the club, when having checked on the errant Chimps next door, I had joined the owners and my self-appointed minder Damian at a table on the club's terrace, drinking-in the twilight atmosphere, one laced with the aroma of fine cigars and eager anticipation that had nightly heralded the start of another adventure. The pre-nocturnal calm was abruptly shattered by the club's dog excitedly alerting us to the arrival of a large brown rat that was sidling casually along the border wall between the club and Bankrobber. The rodent, unperturbed and unfazed by the dog's histrionics, had ambled off into the dark but its appearance had given me pause for thought. For Pest Control to have real purpose, a suitable adversary must surely be a prerequisite.

VERMIN

VERMIN

In an audacious move I had determined to create a quite separate and autonomous authentication board. The premise had been a simple enough one. If Pest Control refused to authenticate street works on the spurious basis that to do so might jeopardize their artist's freedom by opening him to possible prosecution for his much admired acts of vandalism, then what was to stop an independent arbitration board from making a judgement on these works, based on compelling evidential provenance and expertise?

For this to gain credence it would require a respectable platform from which to be launched. This had come in the shape of a long-established Scottish auction house who had been putting together the final cataloguing details for an upcoming sale, a sale that controversially contained many of the contents of the infamous and now sadly deceased Soho drinking den 'The Colony Rooms', a sale most likely inspired by the recent success of Sotheby's 'Pharmacy' auction. More pertinently, they were considering inclusion of a number of street works attributed to Banksy. This had provided a timely and unique opportunity to employ the skills of the hurriedly appointed 'Vermin' board. In return for our expertise, the auction house had agreed that their catalogue would carry an in-depth description of the Vermin board's process and intentions.

So it was, on a glorious morning toward the end of September of that same year, that I had found myself strolling toward the handsome Sir John Soane-designed Church, situated on the eastern most corner of Regent's Park. As I had approached the church, its

Portland stone had glowed reassuringly in the early morning light. The deconsecrated Grade1 listed building had been chosen as the stage for an auction that was to provide the platform for this trial by jury.

Having satisfied myself that the Banksy Lots were all present and correct and after fielding some last minute questions from the auctioneer, and noting a small crowd had begun to gather, I had taken time to cross the busy Euston Road. On approaching the entrance to Great Portland Street station, I had caught sight of that day's Evening Standard banner headline that had read in heavy black capitals

'BANKSY'S, DON'T BANK ON IT!!'

Grabbing a copy from the newsstand and leafing urgently through the pages until reaching a double-page spread featuring the headline.

'THE GRAFFITI ARTIST BANKSY, CAN REVEAL THAT MILLIONS OF POUNDS WORTH OF WORKS ATTRIBUTED TO HIM ARE FAKES'

It would have taken a reader a further eight or more paragraphs to establish that there had in fact been no specific mention of either the auction or its lots, just carefully curated inuendo. A 'coup de grâce', executed with callous and punishing cunning. The damage was done. Not a single Vermin-authenticated work had sold that day or any day since. It was time to take stock and change tack.

THE BUTCHER OF BETHLEHEM

THE BUTCHER OF BETHLEHEM

Bethlehem (/ˈbɛθlɪhɛm/; Arabic: محلتيب Bayt Laḥm) - "House of Meat"

"We can deliver ANYWHERE in the world two works by the most FAMOUS artist in the world just $2 million American dollars for two paintings by the WORLD FAMOUS artist in the world super important works delivered ANYWHERE in the world by the famous artist Bansky!!! - Call George"

So had read the post on the e-commerce platform eBay in the winter of 2008 but the truth was a whole lot more complex. The boastful enthusiasm had certainly been infectious and the ambition whilst absurd had to be applauded, but there had been something in its urgency and agency that had captured my attention. I had been aware of the artist's support for the plight of the oppressed stateless community of Palestine's West Bank but it had all seemed a long way away from the rarified environs of Notting Hill Gate and I had paid it scant regard, that is until my answerphone had been overwhelmed by the excitable and largely unintelligible messages of the post's author, one 'Bethlehem George'.

So it had been to a narrow Bethlehem backstreet, the birthplace of Christ, that the first of the artist's offerings had arrived. To the wall of a humble butcher's shop had been visited 'Stop & Search' a two-metre tall depiction of Dorothy from the Wizard of Oz, dressed in an incongruous pink dress, frisking an armed and uniformed Israeli soldier, his M4 Carbine propped casually against the wall. The butcher had been baffled and bemused by the work's arrival but his neighbour, a humble carpenter by trade, had suggested a solution that might benefit both. He would relieve the butcher of the burden of responsibility of this uninvited offering and in its place build him a much desired and dreamt-of doorway, a structure to reflect the butcher's true stature, a portal to be proud of, one through which his carcasses could be paraded daily. The canny carpenter had been all too aware of the iniquitous nature of this deal but was less certain of quite what to do with the two and a half tons of bricks and mortar, and anxious to avoid the unwarranted attentions of the Palestinian Authority Forces [Fatah] that nightly patrolled the local streets, had hastily cleared a corner of his outdoor workshop to house the two works.

The second of the works 'Wet Dog' had appeared to illustrate an under-dog shaking off the weight of its oppressors in a flurry of Pan-Arabian colours. It had been painted at the site of a disused bus stop within county jurisdiction, but the nature and status of its ownership and acquisition had been less clear and when pressed George had become nervous and agitated. So it was, that with a combined weight in excess of four tons, the two works had sat inert and forlorn, hiding in plain sight amid the chaotic piles of dubious reliquary that marked his trade. For all of George's dreams and schemes, he was at heart a simple carpenter, a cross-maker in a city born of crosses.

Following a frustrating and vexing series of international calls, the two million dollar price tag had dramatically and reluctantly shrunk to a more realistic forty thousand dollars, half of which it had been agreed would be paid in cash on inspection and the remainder paid on the works' safe departure from the Israeli Port of Ashdod. The new price had reflected the inaccuracy of the eBay advertisement that had boasted 'works delivered ANYWHERE in the world by the famous artist Bansky!!!'.

Ignoring the muddled grammatical inference that the artist himself would be the courier, the harsh reality had been that George, for all his childlike optimism, had significantly underestimated the obstacles and impediments inherent in such a promise and clearly the two short journeys from the butcher's shop and bus stop had stretched his logistical capabilities to their limit. It was clear that the works were going nowhere without the intervention of outside forces and had quickly become equally apparent that my usual firm, fronted by the fecund and formidable Sky Grimes, would be neither practical nor appropriate to the task. I had instead employed the skills of a trusted and seasoned war photographer with the role as go-between, a safe pair of hands capable of navigating the perilous and potentially dangerous journey required to secure the two works. The plan on paper was a simple enough one. He was to fly into Tel Aviv and make the thirty-three mile journey across to Jerusalem. From there, after purchasing a local 'burner' phone, he would make contact with George and arrange to meet, inspect and document the works.

The increasingly paranoid George, had chosen the Church of the Nativity in Bethlehem's old town to meet with my agent. This had required him having to make the laboriously slow crossing of the Israel border wall on foot, followed by a brief taxi ride to the old town and finally a short walk to the carpenter's yard, all the while knowing that there were watchful eyes, gunmen and gangsters who would go to great lengths to relieve George of this dubiously acquired contraband.

Satisfied with the works' condition, I had sanctioned the initial payment. Two hundred neatly stacked and folded hundred dollar bills, bound and sealed in an unassuming brown A5 envelope marked with the single word 'Bankrobber', the equivalent of a king's ransom to most of the Palestinian population, but in this instance a deferential down payment that had secured the release of Dorothy and her dog Toto, setting them on a remarkable journey, not along the Yellow Brick Road nor to the Emerald City but one no less eventful, one that would see them cross borders, span oceans and divide opinions.

The works had been scheduled to be loaded onto a flatbed truck during evening prayer to avoid prying eyes and was to be driven by a Palestinian driver to a truck stop in the Neutral Zone at the foot of the division wall, at which point the works were to be craned onto a waiting truck driven by an Israeli driver. A simple enough operation were it not for some seventy years of conflict and mistrust that had made it all but impossible for the two drivers to agree a common consensus on how best to negotiate the handover. This escalated to the point where the operation had been abruptly punctuated by a near-calamitous moment. On being lowered toward the Israeli truck, 'Toto' had slipped her leash in a last act of defiance toward her captors and had crashed to the ground in an explosion of doubt and debris, an unscripted and undocumented event that saw the two warring factions momentarily united in mutual concern. As the dust had settled and it became clear that the work had remained intact, the blame game resumed in earnest, a relentless, seemingly endless, struggle of hubris and pride that continues to play out to this day.

On reaching the border crossing the truck had been approached by an armed Israeli customs officer who had climbed officiously onto the back of the flatbed and on rolling back the tarpaulin, had been met by the vision of 'Stop & Search'. This discovery had been followed by much to-ing and fro-ing by a bemused (and amused) line of border officials in a bizarre choreographed dance of life imitating art, an absurdist photo opportunity unwittingly afforded them by one of their harshest critics.

Banksy's Dorothy and Toto, having been waved through the checkpoint, had begun a journey that would see them set sail from the Port of Ashdod, crossing the Mediterranean into the Alboran Sea, passing through the Strait of Gibraltar into the North Atlantic Ocean, across the Bay of Biscay, then to enter the English Channel, finally docking at Newhaven Harbour, from where it had made the short journey by road to my restorers in rural Kent.

First setting-eyes on the two works, I had been immediately struck by their visceral nature. Running my fingers across the surface of 'Stop & Search' had felt almost spiritual to the touch, the bullet-scarred surface with its ripped and faded remnants, showing the faded faces of the military martyrs and fedayeen who had perished at the hands of their oppressors. Lives lost to a cause fierce fought. It was the first time that I had any real sense of its author's presence or purpose, these works created three thousand miles away in the contested homeland of the Arab Palestinian people. The artist's message of hope hijacked by my own selfish and avaricious intent.

There it was again, that all too familiar pang, that grain of doubt which recedes but never leaves, a haunting maleficent sensation that had stalked me like my own shadow. Not a curse just a question.

The two restored works had travelled some 7,350 nautical miles and a further 1,406 miles haulage by the time they had reached their new home. An epic journey from the dusty back streets of Bethlehem to a shiny Palm Beach palace affording Dorothy and her faithful dog Toto an ocean view to be envied... *"I see skies of blue, clouds of white, The brightness of day, the dark, say goodnight, And I think to myself, Oh, what a wonderful world."*

Pay no attention to that man behind the curtain! He's just a common conman."

The Wizard of Oz.

MONTAUK

MONTAUK

It is August 2011, four years since the ill fated 'Banksy NYC' show and I am sat at the wheel of a 1999 metallic silver Porsche Carrera. Driving east on the Montauk Highway which skirts the southern shoreline of Long Island... I am looking for Jackson Pollock.

I long ago concluded that I didn't much like artists but I had noted it was fifty-five years to the day that this Hamptons' legend had been killed at the tender age of just forty-four, when his baby-blue Oldsmobile Convertible had left the road at speed on a sharp curve heading out of East Hampton, cruelly hurling the artist and his two young female companions into the pages of art history. The car's ad-tag being 'Make a date with a Rocket 88' - a glamorous, if unfortunate boast that bellied the tradgedy of that fatal day.

I had sought a distraction on this bright autumn morning and thought the ghost of a dead artist a suitable companion. It was to be an adventure, aimed at calming my nerves, an excuse to escape the Banksy circus that I had propitiously brought to town. So while its troupe were busying themselves within the cavernous cathedral-like confines of the abandoned Southampton Power Station - soon to be the temporary home to the largest collection of Banksy street works ever shown under one roof... I had determined to make myself scarce.

Driving East on Highway 27, stopping briefly at a couple of roadside bars before collecting my now perennially drunk, spectral passenger from the Blue Parrot Tavern, from whence we had pressed on toward Montauk, passing his homestead studio, purchased with a $5,000 dollar loan from his then patron Peggy Guggenheim, past the site of his fatal car crash, stopping for a reflective beer at Morty's Oyster Stand before proceeding at speed to the easterm most tip of the island where in 1971 Andy Warhol had chanced upon (and subsequently purchased) a small oceanfront estate for just $225,000.

Comprised of five clapboard cottages, it was to become the playground for a litany of the great and the good of Manhattan's elite. Mick Jagger, Keith Richards, Haring, Capote and Jackie Kennedy would all regularly seek refuge here during those long langorous summers of the early seventies.

Finding myself standing suddenly alone, in the shadow of the island's Montauk Point lighthouse, I tried to imagine first Pollock and then Warhol's initial reactions to this mournful windswept landscape. The stark contrast to Manhattan's strictly regimented grid must have felt at once liberating and daunting in equal measure. A landscape unchanged and coldly unconcerned to the trysts and tribulations played out on its foreshore by these hedonistic arrivistes, oblivious to the volitility and drunken rage that had driven Pollock to his death, uninterested in Warhol's petulant and puerile performances, which had pushed Valerie Solanas to empty two rounds into his already frail torso, from her newly purchased .32 Beretta.

The twenty-seven mile return drive from Montauk that evening had given me pause for thought. This was to be my second bite of the 'Big Apple' albeit this time from its rural Long Island cousin. Although the previous NYC debacle had badly bruised my confidence, I consoled myself with the fact that my partner in this second venture had been chosen judiciously. Not this time a pair of scurrilous chancers, rather through the alliance with a pillar of the very community I had mind to plunder. A six foot four inch neoteric wizard, who carried with him an air of confidence that eschewed all doubt, a German émigré of substance, both intellectually and emotionally, whose enthusiasm and energy knew no bounds.

Somewhere between Amagansett and East Hampton I stopped at a roadside cocktail bar, for an ill-advised but locally famous Bloody Mary. Seduced and clearly intoxicated by her charms, I staggered awkwardly back to the borrowed Porsche.

Climbing clumsily behind the wheel, a dense alcohol fog obscuring all logic, the only certainty that now was no time for doubt or deliberation. Stamping hard on the steel accelerator, I sped off into the encroaching night, relentlessly gathering speed. Breaching 110mph on the undulating rollercoaster of a road, I could feel the malevolent twitching black snake of tarmacadam fighting violently to throw me off into the pitch of the night. Determinedly drunk and derelict in my intention, my spectral passenger taunting my every effort to correct the assumed fate.

It was only much later that night, with the silver steed having delivered me safely back to my Hampton hideaway, I reflected that twice since my stateside arrival my fate had been in the hands of Germanic largesse and munificence. Firstly, those of the controversial New York gallerist Stephan Keszler, but more pertinent to that night's adventure, the hands of one Ferdinand Alexander Porsche - the exacting engineer who had unknowingly proved himself my guardian angel.

The distraction had worked... and with all doubt evaporated, the dynamic duo of 'Badman and Robin' was born. The ponies prepared, the clowns calmed, the performance practised, the circus readied.

Roll up, roll up!! Ladies and gentleman, boys and girls, children of all ages, get ready for 'The Greatest Show on Earth'.

GOODNIGHT IRENE

GOODNIGHT IRENE

It is August 18th, 2011, Southampton, New York. "Hi, it's Jon, Jon Bon Jovi," his pistol-grip handshake, firm and reassuring. I'm excitedly engaged in conversation with the New Jersey legend, who is leaning against the hood of his 1970 Chevy Chevelle Ragtop, looking every bit the rock star.

He had been busy congratulating us on our soon-to-be-opened Banksy show and was now animatedly explaining that on a recent flight into East Hampton's executive terminal, he had spotted from the window of his Bombardier Challenger jet a stationary line of traffic snaking its way east out of Queens stretching all along the coastal reach of Long Island. On enquiring, his pilot had explained (without a trace of irony) that this was how people reached the playground of the rich and privileged.

Jon let that sit in the air for a moment before delivering the no-doubt much practiced line, "I didn't even know you could get here by car!"

With a broad smile, the anecdote safely delivered, he effortlessly jumped into his Chevy and was gone, leaving behind him a warm cloud of confidence that was momentarily infectious. Nothing was going to stop this show from being anything less than a wild success.

Three days earlier and some 1,800 miles south of our Long Island location, an unremarkable tropical wave that had formed off the coast of West Africa suddenly and without warning had menacingly changed course and pushed and bullied its way through the

Bahamas leaving chaos in its wake. A dangerous and destructive force of nature hungry for fame and notoriety was hurrying towards us. This subtropical cyclone was officially christened 'Irene' on the eve of our opening reception. The ninth but by far the largest storm of that year's hurricane season and although her name didn't appear on that night's guest list it was clear she had every intention of paying us a visit.

As the VIP guests had started arriving at the 'Old Power Station' situated at 200 North Sea Road, Southampton, I once again felt that nagging kernel of doubt. Was this to be just another misjudged vanity project? The level of wealth of this fashionable enclave became ever more apparent as the evening progressed. Teenagers at the wheels of every conceivable luxury car swerved casually and politely into the hastily enlarged parking lot, but the echoes of New York were already chiming. I watched from the shadows, trying to make out anyone who might conceivably be judged to be a client. The elegant door staff, politely checking off names, had been briefed to indicate the arrival of any celebrity attendance but Irene's imminent arrival had spooked the super-rich into leaving their Long Island retreats whilst they were still able. As the party got into full swing, and the numbers swelled with young, privileged twenty-somethings, across town, the evening sky was punctuated by a steady stream of private jets and helicopters like so many exotic birds hastily making their return migration to Manhattan.

Like Fitzgerald's Gatsby, I was reminded my motives were far from altruistic in their intent. We had set a trap, a glittering jamboree of an affair, aimed at cynically snaring the prize that had continued to evade us. We knew it would take just one person to see past the empty rhetoric of Banksy's Pest Control with their veiled threats and innuendo. But for the moment, I was reminded and reassured by Gatsby's assertion as he had stood alone in the crowd of revellers who mobbed his Long Island mansion, waiting for his Daisy to return to him.

"I like large parties, they're so intimate. At small parties there isn't any privacy."

Like Gatsby, I knew our Daisy was out there somewhere. But that for now all I could do was watch and wait.

The morning after the night before we had woken to bad news. Irene, far from becoming a 'shrinking violet' had grown in confidence and stature and had now reached 'Category 3' on the Saffir-Simpson scale, making her a very dangerous lady indeed. Store holders busied themselves pulling out their storm hoardings and battening down the hatches. There hung in the air an all-pervading sense of anxiety. On visiting The Old Power Station that same morning I had stood in the vast vaulted turbine hall surrounded by the spoils of our plunder and for a fleeting moment had the sense they were mocking me. We had torn them from their homes, dragged them across oceans, paraded them like Victorian freaks, manacled them in chains and restraints for the selfish entertainment of Long Island's elite, humiliated them in a way their author would have found repugnant in the extreme, and now abandoning them to the excesses of a raging harridan that was racing frantically across the Atlantic Ocean like some hysterical avenging angel. And as I pulled the door closed, I thought I could hear the chattering taunts of Banksy's chimps, a scornful screeching cacophony of "Laugh Now But One Day We'll Be In Charge".

AFTER IRENE

AFTER IRENE

"Stop your ramblin', stop your gamblin', stop stayin' out late at night. Goodnight Irene, goodnight"

[Ledbetter & Lomax]

Yes, she had come late to the party but she had certainly made her presence felt, wreaking havoc in her wake, causing damage in excess of $290 million dollars and being directly blamed for 49 fatalities. I had spent that night with my hosts at the Keszler family home, an elegant 1930's shingle-built oasis of calm. Sited within earshot of the Atlantic, it had been carefully designed and built to protect against the most obstreperous and ill-tempered guests and throughout the storm had sat stoic and unmoved by Irene's histrionics.

She had first hit landfall at the eastern tip of Long Island at about 10.00am on that fateful Sunday morning bringing with her gusts in excess of 100mph and for several hours we had listened as she tore through the Long Island landscape in her rabid enthusiasm to reach Manhattan, uprooting trees and smashing down fences like a derailed and demented express train - a Casey Jones on crack.

For our part we had stubbornly defied the call to evacuate and had woken to something resembling a war zone but we were well equipped and climbing into our Mercedes G-Wagon, an all-black 5.5-liter 382-horsepower V-8 engined beast, we set about exploring the extent of our guest's excesses. It had been like navigating a Chinese puzzle or being trapped in some early seventies computer game. We drove down and backed out of countless tree-blocked cul-de-sacs before finally arriving at 200 North Sea Road to bear witness to a bizarre and comically disturbing scene.

The extent of Irene's wrath had known no bounds and in a darkly humorous twist she had taken time to collapse a 200 year-old oak that now lay theatrically across our show's promotional signage, forming an impenetrable wall of branches effectively barring the entrance with a wild roughly hewn portcullis. Once again, we had been stymied in our ambition, not this time by our adversaries at Pest Control HQ but by a greater power. It seemed that even mother nature had taken sides against us, curtailing our endeavours with a blistering natural rebuke - Cosmic retribution writ large.

Bowed but not broken, we looked-on helplessly as the authorities set about the challenge of the big clean-up, an enormous onerous and thankless task that was to dampen any chance of the town returning to normality any time soon. Driving aimlessly about the empty and abandoned streets over the following hours it became apparent that our Banksy show was all but over. Resigned to this truth I had spent the remaining days of my visit drinking coffee, first in the comfort of the Keszler family home then on to the 'Village Gourmet Cheese Shoppe' located on the still boarded-up and largely deserted Main Street. Now a dingy and forlorn place, made gloomy by the hastily installed storm screens, a place that pre-Irene would have been the beating heart of the town, a bright and bustling hub for Southampton's wealthy chattering classes. I would then drive the borrowed Porsche up to the 'Old Power Station' but unlike my earlier pre-storm visits, the shine had gone and the Monkeys were now openly sneering at me, their confidence boosted on having survived Storm Irene unscathed. There had continued to be a steady trickle of curious visitors who filed through the doors of 200 North Sea Road but the wealth had stayed away and the energy had evaporated. It would be a further five days before the evening skies were once more punctuated with the firefly glow of returning jets and helicopters.

Labor day had come and gone, the high season had past and our venture had failed. The evenings were spent in the company of my host, the elegant and erudite art dealer Stephan Keszler and his family. A nightly moratorium would be held at our regular table in the candlelit garden of 'Tutti il Giorno' the towns finest Italian eatery and whilst the mood had been sombre as we had sat counting the cost of the calamitous storm, we drew solace from the dreamy surroundings and became buoyed by the gradual return of the wealth that had been absent for so many days with which our confidence gradually crept back. After all our pitch had been perfect, the presentation faultless and the quality of the works spectacular. That we had failed to find a single buyer, we concluded, could and should be laid firmly at the feet of Irene.

On the last day as I climbed aboard the Hamptons 'Jitney' shuttle bus to begin the long return journey to London I had been overwhelmed by a sense of sadness and impending loss. It had been our second bite of the 'Big Apple's' little cousin and although we hadn't succeeded in our ambition, I realised I had fallen in love with Long Island. Whether riding a borrowed Vespa through Southampton's storm-strewn streets or dining on the ocean-fronting veranda of the towns exclusive 'Bath and Tennis Club' or driving east toward Montauk, speeding past the ghost of Jackson Pollock and on past Warhol's 'Eothen' estate to sit at the base of 'Foulweather Jack's' Cape Byron Lighthouse to just simply marvel at the majesty of the Atlantic Ocean, trying to pick out some vestige of those now long-lost voices of abandon and excess that would have filled the night skies during the heady days of the early seventies, now silenced through the passage of time, replaced only by the deafening hush of immense and unseemly wealth.

I had arrived in the Hamptons broke but full of expectation and enthusiasm and I was set to leave, broke yet paradoxically encouraged. Not knowing then that it would take another fourteen months for a buyer to be found. But on the fifteenth of December 2012, Bansy's 'Stop & Search' was sold by the Keszler Gallery for a high six-figure sum. The spell broken... the curse lifted.

"Goodnight Irene, I'll see you in my dreams".
[Ledbetter & Lomax]

SLAVE LABOUR

SLAVE LABOUR

Julien's Auction House, Los Angeles 15th November 2018. When the hammer came down on Lot no.170, the American artist and self-proclaimed 'propagandist' Ron English, had become the proud owner of one of the most talked-about artworks of recent history. In a hurried press statement, he had vowed to whitewash over his recent acquisition, in a cavalier and puerile protest against the commercialisation of street art.

Stating to a bemused journalist and anyone else who would listen, "We're tired of people stealing our stuff off the streets and re-selling it. So I'm just going to buy everything I can get my hands on and whitewash them out."

Further asserting that his gesture would, "Act as a boon to his good pal Banksy," implying a friendship that seemed as unlikely and hollow as his proposed gesture.

Exactly six years and six months earlier, a small group had gathered around a freshly executed mural applied to the flank wall of a Poundland store in North London's Wood Green in the borough of Haringey. Like wildfire the word had spread that this depiction of a kneeling child hunched over an old fashioned sweatshop sewing machine, slavishly stringing together lengths of Union Jack bunting, was that of the celebrated and much lauded artist and activist Banksy.

Very soon after its arrival, word had reached me that the freeholders of the building were anxious to have a meeting to discuss its removal. It transpired that I had been recommended by the owners of 'No Ball Games' - a work that Bankrobber had successfully removed and were currently representing.

This newly arrived work had however presented me with something of a moral dilemma. I had previously justified the rescue, removal and sale of the artist's works on the grounds that they had either been previously removed by a third party in advance of them coming to Bankrobber, or that they had been deemed to be at risk of being lost to demolition, or council neglect.

But the suggested removal of this newly arrived mural with its paint 'still wet' - a work that had been so warmly embraced by the neighbourhood, had seemed almost vulgar. Worse still, the rumour of its imminent removal had been met with almost hysterical militance.

The building's owners however, had been clearly indifferent to the outpouring of anguish and grief and had presented me with a stark choice. Bankrobber could assist in its removal, for which we would be generously rewarded, or they would have it painted out. This unbending attitude had spurred an ambitious local Labour councillor to step up to the plate and nominate himself as the work's protector.

It had become his own personal cause célèbre and one he pursued with considerable energy and vigour. Journalists relishing the fight had traipsed the traffic-chocked seven mile journey to witness the battle - a David and Goliath encounter, between Banksy's depicted and humbled child busy at his labours pitted against the corporate greed of a North London property developer, aided and abetted by the bad folk from Bankrobber.

If on any given day during that summer of 2012 you had found yourself caught idling in traffic heading northward up Wood Lane, you might well have chanced upon a strange and bizarre scene. That of a small pack of journalists eagerly hanging on the every word of an attention-seeking minor politician. One clearly relishing the unexpected attention. Behind whom, a burly six foot-six security guard, arms folded protectively, stood astride the depiction of a crouched child busying himself at his labours, and in the shadow of this dark sentinel, a distracted and dubious-looking figure dressed in black, rapt in earnest conversation with a jaunty Cork and Kerry plasterer, tape measure in hand and pencil behind ear, busily measuring the required aperture to enable the proposed abduction.

The planned removal was not without risk, bringing with it unprecedented column inches of criticism in both the local and international press, even making the front page of the Financial Times. The schedule had been agreed, the plan actioned. And so it was that some nine months after Banksy's slave child had arrived at its Haringey home, it was unceremoniously hacked from its site and bundled onto the back of a flatbed truck. Broken and blindfolded with a heavy builders tarpaulin, this was the first brutal act of what was to become an elaborate and convoluted game of cat and mouse, that would include an unprecedented transatlantic chase, involving both Scotland Yard and the FBI.

But before any of that could happen, our abductee had to be settled at a safe house deep in the Kent countryside. Here he had been inspected and a schedule of works agreed upon, to clean up the captive urchin and ready him to be paraded in front of what we hoped would be an eager throng of would-be slavers, each vying for ownership.

After two months of painstaking restoration the work was near completion. I had visited the workshop most days during that late summer, watching the progress of the restorers. I had felt like Dickens' Bill Sykes. Remorseless at the theft of the slave child, my initial doubts and concerns toward my actions had all but evaporated with the onslaught that had come my way - a vehement and deafening torrent of abuse from my accusers and haters.

With the restoration complete I had spent the final days of that summer, anxiously stalking the surrounding woodland in the company of my dog Cash, planning, plotting and rehearsing the next stage of the game. Then the all-important news came that my American business partner Stephan Keszler had successfully negotiated the work's inclusion into that year's 'Modern Contemporary and Street Art' sale, a lavish and extravagant event to be held at the prestigious FAAM (Fine Art Auctions Miami) and better still, its director had agreed to enter our slave child as 'Lot no.6' with a generous estimate of $500,000 - $700,000, making it the sale's star-turn and even featuring it as the catalogue's cover. Finally it seemed the tide had turned in my direction.

But back in Haringey, the mood had darkened considerably and their stance had become further entrenched. The local borough council leader's inbox had been overwhelmed with demands to have the work returned and in a bold move she had written to both the Arts Council England and more impressively to the then mayor of Miami, a charismatic ex-news reporter, who had previously covered Angola's civil war and the Soweto riots and who was therefore no stranger to fighting the corner of the underdog. Quite what this Cuban-born political heavyweight, who had interviewed Richard Nixon, Gerald Ford and Jimmy Carter and travelled with presidents Ronald Reagan, George H.W. Bush and Bill Clinton, would have made of the request from a minor British politician to intervene in the fate of a 4ft x 5ft slab of concrete decorated by an anonymous Bristol-born graffiti artist, is anyone's guess. But, just hours before the sale and with thirty potential buyers in attendance and with an initial bid in place of $400,000 - Lot no.6 was dramatically and without warning or reason, withdrawn from sale.

The decision to withdraw the work had been met with jubilation back in Britain, where there had been much back-slapping. The Haringey councillor was able to proudly pronounce to the waiting press that one of the borough's two demands had been met, that the work not be sold, and that the second (that the work be returned) was being stridently advanced.

In Miami, the director of the auction house had issued only a brief statement, saying that he had been inundated by calls and emails from the United Kingdom, many of them abusive and threatening. But he had stopped short of saying that this torrent of abuse had influenced his decision. Privately however he had expressed surprise and indignation at the vociferous and rabid response that the works inclusion had ignited.

Switching the lights off and slamming the corrugated steel door closed shut behind me and with hound to heel, I had pulled the collar of my coat up against the encroaching cold of the evening. For all the headlines and protestations neither Scotland Yard nor the Federal Bureau of Investigation (FBI) had been able to uncover any act of criminality because there had been none. There had only ever been one crime and that had been at the hand of the work's author Banksy.

In the weeks preceding the proposed Miami sale, there had been much speculation as to the work's whereabouts. There had been excited rumours and unsubstantiated sightings. The coffee shops of Miami's fashionable Wynwood Arts District had been awash with tales, there had been talk of a private jet delivering the slave child to the exclusive Miami-Opa Locka Executive Airport, or being chauffeured-in, down through the Florida Keys in a blacked-out limousine, or smuggled in the bows of a private yacht silently navigating its way under Collins Avenue into Miami's Bal Harbour in the dead of night.

The harsh reality was that Banksy's 'Slave Labour' had never made the assumed 4,425 mile trip from North London's Turnpike Lane to Miami's Design District. Rather it had travelled just a paltry sixty-seven miles, first around the busy M25, then pushing out into the Kent countryside along the M2 finally coming to rest at an isolated farm building, where it had remained blissfully unaware of the global fuss and bluster that had followed in the wake of its unwarranted abduction and planned servitude.

LITTLE HOUSE

LITTLE HOUSE

It is January 2013, exactly one month on from the successful sale of Banksy's 'Stop & Search' and I am sat outside No.2 Queen Street, Mayfair, enjoying some rare early morning sunshine and contemplating Bankrobber's next adventure. Across the street a tight huddle of tall darkly dressed men are hurriedly ushering an anxious looking Boris Berezovsky through an open doorway just as the now familiar but no less bizarre sight of art dealer James Stunt's five-car cavalcade sailed past, a $3 million convoy fronted by a brace of Rolls Royce, one a Ghost the other a Phantom, followed by a one-of-a-kind carbon fibre Lamborghini Aventador Roadster, closely tailgated by a pair of blacked-out armour-plated Range Rover Sports. A daily charade that had snaked its way theatrically through Mayfair's narrow streets in an absurd, arrogant and ill-judged show of braggery.

The temperature in the art world had been turned up and crazy had become normalised, the new kids on the block had swagger in abundance and openly craved attention. Gone was the hushed reverence and pained pretension of the Cork Street elite. In its place, a brash new breed who were quite happy to parade and preen like so many Cocks at a fair. These ballers and players, like gate crashers to the party, were hungry for action and were clearly relishing the chase. The previous attendants had been caught sleeping at the wheel and now shocked out of their stupor were quietly and politely appalled at the avaricious intent of their new cohorts. These uninvited guests, largely made up of disbarred and disillusioned ex-city traders, 'Jobbers and Brokers' banished to the wilderness by the ever-tightening grip of the regulators had been searching for a new hunting ground and had chanced upon this gloriously unregulated Garden of Eden with its trees laden with overripe fruit fit for the picking.

Recognising the flaws in the existing and antiquated business model that had remained in place, largely unchanged, for some hundred and forty years, one mired in Victorian values and virtues, an all-male domain, functioning on promissory notes and handshakes, negotiated in fusty old members clubs dotted around St. James and Pall Mall. An old-fashioned and anachronistic model but one which, with a bit of fine tuning, might be profitably adapted to support a new increasingly opaque and murky marketplace.

Gradually and without undue fanfare, a new breed of members' clubs started to appear, replacing the old, dusty establishments with shiny new re-imaginings. Robin Birley's magnificently discreet Five Hertford Street, the bombastic Mayfair Arts Club and a cluster of Nick Jones-inspired private 'houses' - all helped endorse and encourage a veneer of respectability. A smokescreen of opulence built to coax and calm the uninitiated and uninformed, a shiny lure cast across a glassy lake of wealth and excess beneath whose surface dwelt shoals of greedy millionaires and billionaires.

It was to these glistening new theatres of privilege that this breed of self-anointed neoteric wizards would come to practice and hone their dark arts, a small disparate group of adventurers determined on carving out a niche for themselves amid the hubris and extravagance of this exciting new frontier.

It had been only five years since Damien Hirst's Beautiful Inside My Head Forever - a cunningly orchestrated sleight of hand, was staged over two days at Sotheby's West London headquarters. The glitzy star-studded extravaganza had netted the artist a staggering £111million. Considered by many (but never proven) to be a cynical stunt which had coincided, rather too neatly, with the catastrophic collapse of the world's financial markets. Hirst's reported indifference and nonchalance to the commercial crescendo of the venture had resulted in front-page headlines being beamed across the globe.

So when panic gripped the financial industries and redundancies had torn through the city's trading floors like so many forest fires, it was no coincidence that these same headline-stealing boasts captured the imagination of this wandering disparate band of newly-disenfranchised avaricious evacuees, who, on recognising an opportunity, had hastily migrated west to set out their stall. Not this time, in the vertiginous glass towers of Canary Wharf but rather, in the august and hallowed mansions of Mayfair, alongside which, had sprung up vast modernist monoliths built as testament to their creators' wealth and status.

Monuments to Mammon - signalling that an all new 'Art Market' was now open for business.

The billionaire oligarch Boris Berezovsky was found guilty of embezzlement in absentia after publicly falling out with Russia's President Vladimir Putin. He was found dead, in a locked bathroom at his Ascot home on the 23rd March, 2013. Billionaire gold tycoon, playboy and art dealer James Stunt was declared bankrupt on the 6th June 2019.

THIEVES LIKE US

THIEVES LIKE US

It is early spring and I am visiting the London Film Museum, its subterranean entrance tucked away in the south east corner of London's historic Covent Garden. I'm with my logistics team who are assessing the viability of lowering the now crated two tonne work down through the narrow Victorian gated access point. Following the failed Miami sale, quite out of the blue, I had been approached by the owners of the sinisterly named 'Sincura Group' inviting me to consider consigning 'Slave Labour' to their inaugural invitation-only 'Art Event'. The pitch had been very straightforward, the planned event was to feature works by a collection of blue chip artists amongst its number; Damien Hirst, Andy Warhol and Mario Testino. Their proposal was that Banksy's 'Slave Labour' would be the jewel in the crown, a headline-stealing guest, at a party that would culminate in a star studded auction. I would be able to set the reserve, and for their part, they would expect and ask for no financial reward. In the light of this magnanimous offer (and despite some nagging doubts) I had agreed to their terms. After all, I had told myself, where could be the harm in it.

It is Saturday the 1st of June 2013, exactly one year on from 'Slave Labour's' North London debut and a carefully selected group of press had gathered for the great reveal. It was to be the first time the work had received an audience since its controversial abduction. This was to be followed the next day by a champagne soiree for the benefit of Sincura's select VIP clients and set to culminate in a 'Silent Auction' at which enthusiastic attendees would be invited to make offers on the works in the form of sealed bids. I had grudgingly been persuaded to allow the ambitious $1million (dollar) reserve to be announced at the previous day's press call. This had been a decision mired in risk, but I had determined that for the work to achieve the kind of press coverage required to hook a potential buyer, the figure had to exceed all previous headlines. I recognised this had been a gamble but had not counted on quite how big a gamble.

The press headlines had been a disaster. They might as well have screamed 'STOP THIEF!' for the damage inflicted, the first casualty being the immediate loss of the event's champagne sponsor, who understandably had withdrawn their support on seeing the excoriating press coverage of that day. This had been followed by a dramatically dwindling list of VIP attendees as hasty excuses had poured in and feigned apologies proffered.

The promised catering had proved woefully inadequate and the organisation beyond shambolic. It had quickly become clear that my hosts, whilst well-meaning, were hopelessly out of their depth. Perhaps naively they hadn't reckoned on the hostility that the work's inclusion to their event might cause. By midway through that fateful afternoon, they had received their first anonymous death threat, followed by an avalanche of hate mail exacted in a coordinated cyber-attack orchestrated by a team of incensed and angry keyboard warriors. This resulted in their website being at first overwhelmed and eventually paralysed. As the day had progressed, my earlier concern had been replaced by a growing sense of panic. My American business partner, had agreed (with some trepidation) to the work's inclusion, whilst remaining largely blind to the detail. Nonetheless, he had flown over especially to attend the event and had been witness to a scene of such chaos and calamity as to render it almost comical.

The replacement drink sponsor had mysteriously also bailed, leaving the remaining guests hot and thirsty. By early evening the place was emptying at an alarming rate and those that had remained seemed agitated and underwhelmed. Having realised early on, that things were not going well, I had diverted a case of the now vanished sponsor's premier cru to a darkened anteroom. It was to this refuge that I had returned with increasing regularity over the ensuing hours. On returning from one such visit, I had happened upon a scene so disturbing as to render me sober to the spot.

Stood in front of 'Slave Labour', perspiring heavily, was the event's host caught like a rabbit in the headlamps of a sneering and openly hostile film crew, being remorselessly interrogated by a famously pithy BBC arts correspondent who was clearly relishing the intellectual mauling he was inflicting on his hapless prey.

Retreating to the bathroom in an attempt to recalibrate, I had caught sight in the mirror of a familiar face from the near distant past. It was that of the proprietor of the very same esteemed Mayfair Gallery that had robbed me of Banksy's 'Prick' a full four years earlier.

Sensing a change in the power dynamic, I listened as he explained that he had a client interested in 'Slave Labour' and one that was prepared to make an offer on the work. Foolishly emboldened by what I considered my elevated status and with more than a hint of animus, I had explained that the work was to be sold by sealed bids and that at the end of the night I personally would take stock of all the offers and ownership would go to that of the highest bidder. I had arrogantly and recklessly told him, with a fake sense of indifference, that I wouldn't entertain any offer less than one million dollars. This had been followed by a moment's silence. Then turning on his heels and giving away nothing in his countenance, he left as swiftly as he had arrived. leaving me standing stock still, numb and very drunk. Without warning, the door was once again pushed open to reveal my nemesis brandishing a small folded sheet of paper, which he had theatrically pushed into a provided envelope. On handing it to me, he had turned and was gone without pause or ceremony.

Later that evening I had nervously torn open the envelope and unfolded a handwritten note that had read 'My client is prepared to offer $1,000,050 to secure the work known as Slave Labour.'

Five days later, the deal ratified with nothing more than a

handshake and a hangover was done. I had nervously agreed that the work would be moved to a neutral third-party space, after which I was assured the funds would be released to my Bankrobber account. It had been explained, somewhat patronisingly, that this was standard practice in such a transaction. Perhaps foolishly I had decided to keep this transactional detail from my American partner in fear of exposing further incompetence. He had left London in a rage following the Sincura debacle and I was wary of angering him further with the news that I had effectively released our abductee without collecting any small part of its ransom. Walking anxiously through London's Chinatown my phone had lit up with Stephan Keszler's number. My nerves rattled, I had panicked and rashly pushed the 'off' button.

I then stepped into the foyer of the Odeon Leicester Square, purchased a matinee ticket for Baz Luhrmann's newly released 'Gatsby' and waited. The lights dimmed as Jay-Z's polemically pertinent '$100 Bill' had echoed throughout the near empty auditorium.

Two hours and twenty three minutes later as the house lights had lifted to the mellifluous tones of Lana Del Rey's intoxicating 'Young And Beautiful', I had switched my phone back on to the news that a successful transfer of funds of just a hair's breadth over one million dollars had been deposited into my Bankrobber account.

There had only ever been the one offer on that fateful night, but that was all that had been needed.

[SLAVE LABOUR] Stencil & Spray Paint on render and brick - Sold $1,000,050

NO BALL GAMES

NO BALL GAMES

The headline had read 'Thieves Steal Banksy Art'. For as far back as I can remember I have had an aversion to authority and hypocrisy. It had been six years since that first ill-considered call had come through admonishing and rebuking me for my actions. The call that had started the ball rolling. That had put the game in play. Without that initial rebuke would I have had the appetite, inspiration or enthusiasm to board the rollercoaster that had followed? A high-stakes game of cat and mouse that would span more than a decade, costing thousands of dollars and gambling millions more, splitting global opinion with a series of divisive gestures of presumed thievery, which had flown in the face of the artist's wishes, resulting in a deluge of criticism and scorn.

Looking to replicate the successful sale of 'Slave Labour', I had (with some reservation) agreed to entertain the invitation to consign to the (now annual) Sincura Group art event. I had once again been charmed and disarmed by its hosts' verve and infectious enthusiasm. They had explained that this event was set to eclipse its predecessor in both scale and ambition. It had been billed as an unparalleled extravaganza, featuring the largest collection of Banksy Street Works ever displayed under one roof. The roof in this instance was that of the newly opened luxury Melia ME Hotel situated on the site of the now demolished Gaiety Theatre where the Aldwych meets the Strand, a theatre famed for its 'Gaiety Girls' and more pertinently for staging the 1931 hit musical 'The Millionaire Kid'. I don't recall why I had let this deeply buried fact colour my judgement but in spite of my reservations, I had agreed to once again throw my hat into the ring. Confident in the knowledge that the devil takes the hindmost, I had reluctantly agreed to consign the newly restored 'No Ball Games' to this well-intentioned circus.

After all, I had told myself, what is the worst that can happen.

Turning off the southernmost stretch of the Aldwych on a beautiful spring morning, I found that I had arrived just in time to find my 'fixer' Sky (and his team) readying themselves to leave, their trucks access to the subterranean entrance having been blocked by an overly officious security guard sporting a clip board and a blinding hi-vis jacket.

Quickly I established that an edict from above had been issued, that no works were to be granted access to the hotel's property until such time that an outstanding bill be settled. My agreement to consign had been based on the understanding that we were to be the event's lauded hosts, the star turn, the main attraction at this circus of insincerity. The realisation that we were in fact,to be little more than 'paying guests' had filled me with trepidation.

On hearing this unexpected news, I should have turned tail and bowed out gracefully with my reputation at least nominally intact. It was in that moment of indecision, that a huge lumbering figure had emerged from out of the dark cavernous depths of the hotel. Devil, a 'Close Protection Officer', tasked with looking after the show's assets. At just shy of seven feet tall, he was a black mountain of a man with the studied forbearance of someone who could make light of any problem. With his penetrating stare and a grin that at once reassured and threatened, he was the perfect antidote to my fears. I was instantly convinced that for as long as I remained in this man's orbit, surely no ill could befall me. In his wake all doors and channels would open, the petty politics of the hotels bureaucracy had simply evaporated in his presence. It was not, as might be supposed, his physical presence that so disarmed, rather it was his childlike countenance that had the effect of neutralising all hostility. Devil belied his name by being to all intents and purposes a two hundred and fifty pound man-child whose charismatic and open charm floored all and any attempt to provoke confrontation. The devil in this instance was not so much in the detail as in the delivery.

The journey that had brought me to this place and in the company of this particular work, if measured in miles, had been few but it had been a significant one nonetheless. The call to arms, like others before, had come through the now familiar network of North London property developers that seem to have unwittingly fallen prey to Banksy's pen. Far from feeling singled-out or persecuted, the Orthodox community had enthusiastically embraced this new and unexpected revenue stream and had delighted in the artist's uninvited attentions. So it was in an extraordinary gesture of trust that the beneficiaries of 'No Ball Games' had afforded Sky and myself a rare insight into their world. We were to be their honoured guests, invited to break bread and conclude the delicate and critically discreet business of removing and selling the work on their behalf. Delicately and discreetly we had arrived, in what Sky had later explained as having been a tactical manoeuvre, rattling through the streets of their North London enclave at heart-stopping speed in his newly acquired 220k fully-loaded Ferrari Spider 458, coming to an abrupt halt in a dramatic cloud of gravel, dust and cigar smoke. The youngsters, clearly impressed by this vulgar display of wealth, had gathered around the car excitedly whilst our hosts inured and mildly irritated by this uncouth display of Mammon had proceeded to give us a tour of their facilities which had included a dedicated ambulance service with its own fully integrated call centre, aimed specifically at protecting their womenfolk from requiring assistance from a non-orthodox crew. They had gone on to explain that theirs was a proudly closed-knit community, built on firm values and a stoic sense of self, best illustrated when one of their elders had seized the opportunity to regale us with a tale from the recent Tottenham riots, boasting that one of their number, a flame haired colossus had single handedly halted the venomous tide of vitriol and hate as it had surged tirelessly toward them. The message delivered was subtle but clear, they were not to be messed with, their genteel persuasion not to be confused as weakness and that for all our West London bluff and bluster, this was to be a simple business transaction - and one to be conducted by their rules.

"They tried to kill us. They failed! Now, we eat." It was in this spirit that we had retired for lunch.

What followed was a two hour crash course in Judaism, during which I had clumsily attempted to navigate my way through the requisite do's and don'ts of their ancient credo. Our hosts had presided over the proceedings with considerable patience and calm in spite of Sky's natural exuberance and charm, having ricocheted recklessly around the restaurant forcing their wives into a canny dance of manners to avoid his relentless and teasing attention.

As a lapsed Catholic I had some sense of religious etiquette but within the confines of their tightly structured rituals, I was hopelessly out of my depth, unsure if the bowls of water that had been ceremoniously bought to each placement between courses were to wash one's hands or to drink from. Having tripped at every hurdle and with lunch complete, there had followed a long and drawn-out period of negotiation, littered with mangled manners and muddled metaphors, a meeting that had veered frenetically from the awkward to the absurd. Like a pair of Buddhists at a Bar mitzvah, we had struggled to find any common ground or agreement. It was clear that the shear heft and scale of the work presented such logistical costs as to make its removal all but untenable.

Finally in the spirit of compromise it was agreed that for this particular wall of Jericho to be tamed and tailored to our mutual benefit, we must employ the judgement of Solomon, separating the mischievous and errant adolescents by the application of a number of judicious and carefully considered cuts.

Leaving North London in the late afternoon sun, subdued and humbled by the day's proceedings, I had been struck by the notion that for a brief moment we had been the outliers, the subject of scrutiny, suspicion and curiosity and I could not help but wonder at the tenacity of spirit required to endure and maintain such a faith.

The following Sabbath, three of Sky's finest, armed not with trumpets and faith but diamond-tipped chain saws and brawn, had set about the task of dismantling Jericho. Choosing midday of the hottest weekend of that year, had been a tactical decision aimed at reducing unwarranted attention. The rationale being that the majority of North London would be slaving away at their barbecues or basking in their gardens and parks rather than angrily picketing a busy and congested intersection.

Dressed in balaclavas and heavy white boiler-suits, their cuffs and ankles taped tightly to protect against the impending dust storm, they had set about the extraction, but within minutes had found themselves bundled into the back of a Black Mariah and on their way to being charged with malicious damage.

It transpired that there had been one major flaw in their plan, yes there had been few people about on that hot afternoon and the traffic had been light and largely uninterested, but remarkably they had overlooked the large bank of CCTV cameras that had bristled cartoonishly above them, a live feed directed to the screens of the local constabulary. There had followed a slew of urgent calls as we had tried to locate the missing crew to secure their release, a task considerably hindered by the building owners' resolute and unyielding observance of shabbat. Three hot hours later the 'Haringey Three', as we had dubbed them, were reluctantly freed with charges pending, only to have them quietly dropped on the completion of the Sabbath.

The exhibition 'Stealing Banksy' had been roundly criticised and condemned by both the press and the artist's representatives and had yet again failed to find a single buyer but was nevertheless attended by more than ten thousand enthusiastic visitors over a three-day period. In response to the exhibition a spokesperson for the artist had issued the following statement.

Banksy would like to make it clear - "This show has nothing to do with me and I think it's disgusting people are allowed to go displaying art on walls without getting permission."

Six months on from the 'Stealing Banksy' show, I had received a flurry of texts from the owners of 'No Ball Games' alerting me to the breaking news that Banksy had been reportedly arrested. An American news website had alleged that the identity of the British street artist had finally been revealed following his arrest in the London borough of Watford, where he was being held "Without bail on charges of vandalism, conspiracy, racketeering and counterfeiting". The story claimed that at the location of his arrest, "thousands of dollars of counterfeit money along with future projects of vandalism" had been found. The owners, clearly uninterested as to the artists plight, had wanted to know only one thing, had the unveiling of the artists true identity reduced or increased the potential worth of their investment? One glance at the clumsily constructed arrest photograph had satisfied me that the report was an obvious hoax, but their question had been a reasonable one and one that I had wrestled with from the beginning of my journey. Just how much of the artists success had been as a direct result of his artistic competence, compared to that of his fiercely protected anonymity? Had Bruce Wayne dismissed his trusty butler Alfred or Peter Parker swept away his cobwebs or Don Diego De La Vega's 'Zorro' cast aside his famed rapier or Robin Hood acceded to the will of his Sheriff?

Banksy, I had concluded, could by the simple act of unmasking himself, demolish in one stroke the very edifice of greed he so railed against, an edifice cunningly constructed and maintained to shield that same anonymity, one that had been slavishly supported by the auction houses and galleries, all kowtowing to the artist's micro-managed demands. No other artist before or since has inspired such rabid loyalty from so many for so little. Was, after all, his work really on balance that of a modern day genius, or was it his meticulously maintained anonymity that marked out his true talent? Would the often trite motifs and protestations of a forty-five year old Bristolian caucasian male really inspire such religious fervour were it not for the mystery, and the societal amnesia and mass denial that had held his audience in thrall to this day? To protect the seemingly impenetrable veil of secrecy that surrounds the legend that is Banksy. A Robin Hood for our times. One "To be feared by the bad, and loved by the good, Robin Hood, Robin

Hood...... Robin Hood."

'No Ball Games' was removed in three parts over a three-day period. It remains unsold, caged and incarcerated in three sturdy wooden crates at a Long Island lock-up, its children cruelly separated, their rebellious spirit crushed., entombed in a pointless, sad, reverie of loss.

It has become clear in recent years that 'No ball games' signs are not effective in preventing young people from playing with balls in residential areas. [Haringey Council]

SHEPHERD MARKET

SHEPHERD MARKET

I had first been made aware of this neighbourhood when at one of my many Saturday surgeries, a young man had visited Bankrobber's Notting Hill space carrying an unpromising canvas backpack, out of which he had produced a tatty length of torn blanket, unfurling it to reveal what he told me was an original Banksy. The clumsily, and no doubt, hastily removed panel of wood featured a small stencilled rodent, sat on its haunches furtively glancing over its shoulder, whilst clasping an intrusively long lensed camera. He had gone on to explain that the piece had formed part of a dilapidated door on a derelict building in Shepherd Market and that his research had pointed to it being one of a number of well documented Banksy works known as 'Paparazzi Rats' that had been recorded around West London. I had mistakenly taken him to mean Shepherd Bush Market, but on further enquiry I had found myself directed to a hidden and largely ignored Dickensian backwater situated at the southernmost corner of Mayfair, flanked to the west by Park Lane and with Picadilly to its south.

I had first approached this neighbourhood on a grey London morning, having turned north off Piccadilly into the darkly atmospheric White Horse Street, a narrow soot-stained thoroughfare, where on reaching its halfway point, it had revealed a London seemingly unchanged since the middle of the 18th century. It had been like walking into the opening scene of Carol Reed's musical 'Oliver', an extravagant bustling hive of activity with a myriad of tiny cafes and bars catering for all tastes and types, all enthusiastically vying for the attention of the wealthy clientele that had been congregating here for more than two hundred years, the discreetly attendant coachmen atop their gleaming black carriages of old now replaced by Ray-Ban wearing, dark-suited athletically built chauffeurs keeping hawkish watch over their masters. In recent years the Market with its uniquely restricted access had become a popular destination for millionaires and billionaires, a discreet village set within the very heart of Mayfair, its unique geographical situation coupled with the reassuring presence of a visibly armed diplomatic protection corps assigned to the nearby Saudi Arabian Embassy that patrolled the surrounding streets with a metronomic regularity, creating a plutocratic oasis of wealth.

By the time I had arrived at the original site of the 'Paparazzi Rat', the building was already well on its way to becoming Mayfair's most exclusive nightspot. But for now was shrouded in scaffolding awaiting its grand reveal. It was not immediately clear why Banksy had chosen No.6 Trebeck Street to site this particular rodentine offering. It was true that the neighbourhood had a reputation, considered as it was by many to be Soho's sophisticated cousin and it certainly had the type of camera-shy clientele that would be regularly targeted by the gutter press. But for as long as anyone could remember this particular building had been the site of an eccentric Victorian-style eating house that had fallen into dereliction and had lain abandoned and neglected since its closure in the late nineties. Strangely ignored and normalised in its decay amid the surrounding affluence.

But in late 2012 in a bold gesture to take back the crown of his late father Mark Birley, the celebrated and much lauded founder of Annabel's Nightclub, his son Robin, the heir apparent to the Mayfair club empire, had taken on this broken down building along with several adjacent properties on Trebeck and Hertford Street to create '5 Hertford Street', an exclusive private members club, that upon having opened had quickly become the talk of the town. Billionaires and millionaires rubbing shoulders with politicos and royals, it was a magnet to the rich and famous. With its anonymous understated exterior and warren of opulently decorated lounges and dining rooms, it had become an instant success providing an ultra-private environment where discreet deals could be done and liaisons ratified without fear of recrimination or report. With deals settled and bids sealed, members and their guests were invited to descend into the dimly lit recesses of the building, a lavish and sumptuous maze of bars and dance floors that formed 'Loulou's' nightclub, a fantasy-filled extravaganza where the rigours and rules of upstairs were relaxed to encourage a bacchanalian atmosphere of well-mannered excess. Within these hallowed chambers could be found short exaggeratedly tanned men dancing with exotic vertiginous blondes whose sexual ambiguity only added to the frisson. The democracy of wealth and beauty blurred into a vortex of enthusiasm and excitement where subtly nuanced nocturnal arrangements were brokered and broken in a helter-skelter of hedonistic haste.

On one occasion attending a friends birthday party, I recall seeing the celebrant slumped at a table in quiet reverie, when she was suddenly overwhelmed by a nauseous and immediate need to vomit. Unable to stand, she had relented to the urge where she sat. Immediately out of the darkness had sprung a team of pen-torched helpers who gently and seamlessly propped her back up into her seat, hastily cleaning and removing any evidence of the unwelcome aberration, then immediately retreating invisibly back into the shadows, leaving her pride intact, for all the world as if nothing untoward had occurred. On another occasion, after a long languorous lunch had spiralled inadvertently out of control, lurching into a herculean epic of excess that had stretched long into the night, I had settled to rest awhile under the kind and watchful gaze of the club's resident giraffe only to awake some hours later to find myself surrounded by a coterie of patient and purposeful staff, who on my waking, had jumped to attention, helping me on with my coat, straightening my collar whilst studiously hunting down my bowler hat. Then politely and without any sense of rancour or ill will, had politely ushered me out into the coming dawn. One had the firm sense that within the cloistered confines of the club's walls no harm could befall you, no indignity consume you, no judgement define you. In contrast, the architect of this nightly carnival was, like Fitzgerald's Gatsby, a somewhat diffident host preferring to sit back and observe from the shadows in the quiet contemplative company of his wistful whippets, a reserved and remote master to all he surveyed. The King of Clubs in his house of cards.

So it was in an ironic twist of fate, that where once had stood the doorway to a derelict Victorian eatery, also the original site of Banksy's prying rodent, there now existed a smartly painted unremarkable door, but for a small brass plaque that read 'Cigar Room'. A door through which, members and their guests could discreetly come and go, unnoticed and unimpeded by the prying attention of the waiting paparazzi that had nightly stalked the club's main entrance since its inception. Had Banksy had a cosmic premonition on that night six years earlier, a clairvoyant moment that had bought him to this particular portal through time and space? An urban instinct that had inadvertently led to a triumvirate of Robins to momentarily exist at the same geographical location, our footsteps crossing through time, layered upon all those that had trod before us, a psychogeographical signpost into the future.

Excited at the prospect of the club's imminent addition to the neighbourhood, I had decided to set up shop as close to this new arrival as possible. 'Bankrobber Mayfair' was to be a cunningly sited honey trap from which I would ensnare this new wealth, I'd convinced myself it would be like shooting fish in a barrel. Almost without trying I had chanced upon a small empty shop on the southern aspect of the market that had until recently been a toy emporium dedicated to the selling and restoring of lead soldiers, a place where battalions of brightly painted troops and platoons of mounted cavalry had lined the shelves with swords drawn and bayonets fixed, in a defiant but historically absurd standoff, an archaic remnant of a bygone age, a place where, for generations, the upper-classes when bringing their reluctant sons to the market to introduce them to the pleasures of carnal contact, might visit the shop to stare dewy-eyed through its window like their fathers before them, or perhaps to deposit a shoe box of lovingly wrapped memories for restoration at the hands of the two fastidious brothers who had run the shop with an almost religious rigour over many years. Boy to man and back to boy in a seemingly endless cycle of privileged paralysis, one blind to the winds of change that had swirled restlessly through the neighbourhood over recent years. And now with their grown-up sons conscripted to the city or civil service, the visits had slowed to the point where the brothers were left with little choice but to reluctantly shut up shop. The battlefields laid bare, the cannons silenced, an era ended.

After a seven-day dash to meet the rigorous demands of the landlords, a lease on No.5a Shepherd Street had been secured. This had been followed by an extensive and expensive refurbishment during which, on one of my many site visits, I had found the small ground floor piled high to the ceiling with rubble, looking for all the world as if a house had been demolished locally and its remains barrowed irreverently into my empire of dirt.

From the off I had in mind to create two very different environments within the tiny space. At street level with its polished concrete floor and deep-red painted walls, it would feature a single floor-to-ceiling pane of bandit-proof glass which was to act as a window into the world of Bankrobber, a place where bait would be tethered like a goat to a post, a lure set to tempt and entice the cash-burdened rich that would nightly prowl the streets of the market only to be drawn in by the window's rebellious glow like so many moths to the flame.

In sharp contrast, the lower ground floor that had once served as a field hospital to the wounded and weary foot soldiers of its previous tenants, had been fashioned into a private clubroom accessed by a narrow dog-leg staircase which had creaked theatrically, then opening onto a dark subterranean den lined with full-length oak panelling, and underfoot an ancient ebony parquet floor. A room of pure fiction, illuminated only by a brace of brass wall sconces featuring blindfolded cherubs holding aloft dimly lit incandescent candle lights. A lie that gave the illusion to having been there forever, an intimate arena from which to practice the dark arts of 'Turning Rebellion into Money'.

Exactly two months after putting my signature to paper, on the 4th July 2013 'Independence Day' Bankrobber Mayfair was ready to open. The trap readied, the stage set.

But as summer had turned to fall of that year, it quickly became apparent that I had made a grave error of judgement. The space had indeed been perfect, situated as it was just fifty yards from Hertford Street and a similar distance from Curzon Street known locally as 'Hedge Fund Alley', but I had overlooked two fundamental truths. The first being, that the super wealthy don't amble or browse, they do not stray from their purpose, making only the necessary few steps required to reach the entrance to their club from their blacked-out carriages and repeating the same journey at the end of each evening. The second being that those aspiring to become super wealthy had neither the time nor inclination to dawdle, making only the necessary few steps to join the lineups of the takeaway food outlets that lined Curzon Street, then immediately returning to their avaricious endeavours, chained to their purpose and on the close of each trading day swarming thirstily to the nearest pub to drink and dissect the days dealings. The dawning of these two truths had sat heavy with me during the summer of 2013 and although loving my new space, I had become resentful of the tyre-kickers and time-wasters that would seek me out. Saturday mornings had become purgatory. The very same people who had plagued me with their tales of 'Banksy's that had got away' and opportunities missed were now making the exodus from the rarified environs of Notting Hill. In a weekly pilgrimage of pointless platitudinous piety, they had arrived at my door. I had once again begun to feel less like an art dealer and more like a priest, reluctantly running a weekly confessional. Resentment was soon replaced by rage, an internalised sensation of self-loathing at my own stupidity, how could I not have seen the obvious? After all, I had witnessed it before, long ago in those early unregulated City trading days. The ethos of those brash 'Loadsamoney' foot soldiers of the late eighties had simply been refashioned and tailored to suit these new times. Less vulgar? Yes!... but fundamentally the same. They had no time then and they had no time now for the distraction and frippery of art.

In my enthusiasm during the weeks prior to the opening of Bankrobber Mayfair, I had added a few finishing flourishes commissioning a number of ornate stained-glass panels to decorate the door's entranceway in an allegorical illustration of intent. The main piece, featuring a pair of crossed pistols circled with the words 'Turning Rebellion Into Money' with Dollar, Euro and Yen symbols swirling upwards from the smoking barrels. Separately and to each side a latticework of panes featuring wildly decorated iridescent snakes and ladders in a contemporary reimagining of the children's game of fate and fortune, but the pièce de résistance had been an electronically operated blind that stretched the full height and width of the picture window. Fashioned from bible black cloth and featuring a large gold depiction of Elvis Presley's favoured handgun, an elaborately decorated 'Colt Python' with the inscription 'TCB' carved into its stock and running below the length of its barrel in gold letters the words 'Taking Care of Business.', the King's signature catchphrase and one that I had appropriated as Bankrobber's own.

In those early hope-filled halcyon days, I strode purposefully down White Horse Street with a spring in my step, jostling cheerily past the ghosts and spirits that had frequented this ancient thoroughfare for more than two centuries and on approaching 5a Shepherd Street, the blind as if by magic would gently lift to present the day's reveal. But by the onset of that same winter my mood had darkened considerably, the purposeful stride replaced by an anxious gait. My journeys down White Horse Street now impeded by the sharp elbows and shoulders of its past inhabitants. I would find any excuse to avoid Bankrobber, favouring instead the cloistered comfort of the nearby 'Little House' members club with its log fires, velvet couches and congenial atmosphere. Increasingly the blind had remained down, at first for hours of each day and then by days of each week and then more recklessly by weeks of each month. The jokey benign message that at first had hinted at exciting things to come, looked ever more malign as time had passed. Like Heller's 'Major Major' from Catch-22, I had favoured absence and obfuscation over truth and reality. It's true that I had attempted a couple of exhibitions in the months leading up to Christmas of that year but rather than playing the role of enthusiastic host I had turned into a surly spectator, choosing instead to watch the proceedings from a darkened doorway opposite. On the one occasion I did attend one of my own events, it had ended disastrously in a near fistfight. The role of Ringmaster rapidly and without warning, turned to that of clown.

Turning onto White Horse Street one rain soaked December night, I had been confronted by a strange and unexpected sight. Where only the day before there had been nothing more than some broken down hoardings, now stood the newly arrived and freshly painted facade of 'Hatchetts Restaurant and Bar'. At first, I had taken it to be a hallucination, a mirage conjured to taunt me by the malevolent forces that seem to have taken over of the street of late. But on entering I had been greeted warmly by its proud owner who had proceeded to give me the grand tour. Enthusiastically walking me through the ground floor bar, with its deep red painted walls and exposed brickwork, then down a sweeping stairway that opened dramatically onto a vast dimly lit cavernous dining room with its walls washed with platinum and gold leaf. It had struck me as being a reassuringly auspicious addition to this otherwise darkly disturbed thoroughfare and more importantly a much needed boost to my fast failing mood. Standing alone at the empty bar on that first night, staring at my reflection looking back at me from the optic ladened mirrored wall, I had thought myself like Kubrick's 'Jack Torrance' trapped in a cashless stasis, unable to move forward and unwilling to look back. I had left that night both pleasantly intoxicated and emotionally emboldened, convinced that this new addition to the market must be an augur to good fortune, an extraterrestrial gift that both looked and felt like Bankrobber but with the significant advantage of not actually being Bankrobber.

I had later discovered that the original incarnation of Hatchetts sited a few hundred yards away on Piccadilly had been the fashionable seventies hangout for the glitterati of the day, one regularly visited by amongst others Adam Faith and The Rolling Stones. So this latest incarnation with its well-stocked bar and vexingly vague staff had provided me with the perfect excuse to avoid Bankrobber altogether, studiously rationing my visits to times I could be certain that there was little or no chance of meeting anyone.

It transpired that the warm welcome that had greeted me on that first rainy night had belied a more complex situation and one that went some way to explaining the sudden arrival of this swiftly assembled apparition. The smiling and enthusiastic young man who I had taken to be the owner, was in fact the son of the owner. The father in contrast, a colourful vaudevillian character, part gangster, part raconteur who, on having ceremoniously handed over the reins to this poisoned chalice, injudiciously proceeded to hold court from its most prominent table, leaving its charming but hapless host hopelessly adrift, the captain at the helm of a doomed ship. Mayfair's own Mary Celeste, swept in by an ill wind and now trapped in a stagnant dark backwater. The 'gift-horse turned albatross' had quickly become home to a ragtag group of small-time crooks, transvestites and scurrilous drunks, whose vulgar Hogarthian behaviour ensured that during the day the place had remained largely empty but come nightfall its mood would darken significantly, lurching violently between high spirits and low morals.

Not since the days of Jack Leach's Gas Works restaurant, had I found myself in such extraordinary and disquieting company. It quickly became apparent that this most recent manifestation of Hatchetts had been created as a dubious respite, a watering hole for the derelict and dispossessed where cheap tricks were turned and debts settled, a shambolic Shangri-La for the damned and disaffected.

Comfortable in these new surroundings and enjoying the anonymity bestowed upon me by its disparate rabble. I had set about planning my next move. I had thought myself playing Monopoly, arrogantly positioning myself on the board's dark blue square and waiting for the money to roll in. Then suddenly and without warning I had found myself tumbling chaotically down the diamond decorated back of the new game's longest snake. Forced to roll the dice and start again. For seven years I had been climbing ladders and enjoying the spoils along the way but I had become complacent and had lost sight of my purpose. The expected cash cow had turned into a white elephant, a pallid pachyderm that I had dragged to market and that now sat dormant, shamed and shielded behind Bankrobber's bible black blind. Silenced like a canary in its cloth-covered cage, out of sight and out of mind.

GIRL WITH BALLOON

GIRL WITH BALLOON

With the blind now permanently down and the bait long since perished, it had become clear that Bankrobber had not only failed in its boast of "Turning rebellion into money," but it had manifestly and recklessly neglected its twin boast, "Taking care of business". Perhaps too late, I realised that it was the cat-and-mouse-game that had been the life-blood of Bankrobber. Spurred-on by the sale of 'What?' and the ensuing capers, culminating in the one-million-dollar sale of 'Slave Labour'. In short, without Banksy there was no Bankrobber.

A lifeline had come in the form of an unsolicited invitation to inspect what had been described as one of the artist's most recognised and iconic images. This particular rendition of 'Girl With Balloon' had languished unseen and unnoticed behind an advertising hoarding in East London since its execution in 2006. A site visit had revealed a sad and forlorn specimen, with peeling paint and six years of urban grime obscuring its whimsical charm. The freeholders of the building, a pair of Orthodox Jews, had heard of our previous exploits and were keen to employ our services.

Satisfied with our terms, and with due diligence observed, Sky and his cohorts had set about planning its removal. Unlike previous extractions, there had been no expectation of protestations or press due to it having had no public presence. As a result I had considered my usual role, as agent-provocateur (one that I so relished) would be an unnecessary distraction on this occasion and chose to stay away, So it was with a degree of trepidation, that I had set out for Q Scaffolding's West London headquarters, uncertain of what I might find. Sky, keen not to attract prying eyes, had instructed that I access the premises by a convoluted and circuitous route, which had involved me having to scramble over a mountain of debris, then finally to pull back a stubborn curtain of rusty corrugated sheet allowing me to squeeze awkwardly and inelegantly into the yard. From the superior look on Sky's face I rightly surmised that this was his way of reprimanding me for my absence at the time of the works removal - a reminder, if one was needed, as to who was the real boss. I had, in effect, been made to use the tradesman's entrance. Satisfied with the rebuke he had proceeded to lead me to a corner of the yard where there stood an unpromising pile of rubble stacked precariously onto a pair of broken pallets with a tarpaulin hastily concealing what I took to be the painted surfaces but on pulling back the cover I could only stare incredulously at four seemingly blank slabs of filthy brick-backed render, the raw edges of which spoke to the brutal manner of their extraction. Sensing my dismay and disappointment he ordered one of his team to clean one of the slabs, the hapless lackey eager to please had plunged a stiff brush into a nearby bucket of stagnant water and proceeded to vigorously scrub away at the renders surface, assuring us in his broken English that it was 'just dirt boss, not a problem, just dirt'.

The owners, anxious to evidence their investment in its removed state, had pushed hard to see the work, threatening to withhold funds for the much needed restoration until such time that they were satisfied with its safe and satisfactory extraction. Determined to avoid such a meeting in light of the works shocking condition, I had tactfully explained that a weekday visit was inadvisable as the incongruous sight of a pair of Orthodox Jews scrambling through Sky's West London wasteland would risk attracting the very attention they were so very anxious to avoid, certain in the knowledge that their observance of Shabbat would make a weekend visit all but impossible. The pair snookered by their faith had reluctantly released the required funding, enabling the work in its sad and sorry state to make that now familiar journey down the M2 toward rural Kent unchecked and unseen.

Caveat Emptor. Writ large.

Daily, during that summer, I had made the short trip to the restorers from my coastal retreat, a small single-story black shiplap property, perched high above the shingle foreshore of North Kent, a bleak estuarine escape situated at the point where the River Thames meets the sea, where, for centuries, at the turn of each tide, it had emptied its malodorous miasma of memories onto the intertidal mudflats, the gentle ebb and flow, sifting through the secrets and sins of generations of Londoners past and present, leaving its haunted waters to wash gently over the dark Dickensian landscape.

With its proximity to the city, this desolate and neglected backwater had proved the perfect hideaway, one that had served as home to generations of London's most notorious gangsters and villains. The Krays, Richardsons, Noyes and Knights had all set out their stall in this overlooked corner of Kent, its local golf club openly boasted of its role in the planning and execution of many of the great bank robberies and heists of recent history. So I had thought it an ironic and fitting tribute that this, the final caper, should be curated and coordinated from my coastal cliché.

My restorer's initial despair on seeing the state of the work had been quickly allayed by his team's infectious enthusiasm, the painstaking application of thousands of dampened cotton buds applied over hundreds of hours had gradually revealed the artists original intention. The mauled and mangled render lovingly stitched back together to create a seamless recreation of the artist's original canvas whilst skillfully managing to maintain the work's urban integrity.

The return journey from rural Kent to Mayfair had been an unremarkable one but on arriving at 5a Shepherd Street it became clear that in my determination to maintain the work's authenticity, I had made a glaring oversight, a schoolboy error that had resulted in the crated work being precisely five inches taller than the door's aperture. The two tonnes of lovingly restored bricks and mortar set within its handsome bespoke steel frame, that had spun balletically from the restorer's gantry, its block and chain suspension lending it the grace and ease of a practiced trapeze artist had, on being unceremoniously deposited on the pavement of Shepherd Market, reverted to type and presented a more stubborn and churlish character trait, that of precisely what it was - a two-tonne slab of bricks and mortar, which now stood rooted to the spot, anchored only by gravity and grit.

Whilst the Market was no stranger to calamitous intrusion it was evident that this newly arrived monolith was already drawing a good deal of unwanted attention. To make things worse, as I had sat at the window of the ironically named 'L'Artiste Muscle' (an eccentrically staffed steak restaurant sited opposite Bankrobber) the heavens had unexpectedly opened, causing harsh curtains of heavy rain to dash angrily at the crate's surface, as if in protest. Following several urgent calls (and the promise of half a dozen large servings of steak and chips) a team of 'Q' liveried scaffolders had descended on the market and proceeded to undress the work where she stood. Stripped of her protective armour, the vulnerable work with its whimsical message of hope, looked momentarily dejected and forlorn but with the ingenious and harrowing application of some short lengths of scaffolding pole and a not inconsiderable amount of brute force, Banksy's 'Girl With Balloon' had been coaxed and cajoled onto her new stage, awaiting the limelight by the very same team that had dragged and manhandled her from her East London sojourn. The four mile journey across London, punctuated by a three month coastal convalescence costing thousands of pounds, had left my nerves frayed and my wallet once again empty. So as I sat alone at that restaurant table on that early autumn evening, I had taken a moment to ponder the synchronicity of it all. Less than twenty yards and more than twelve years on from when Banksy had first come to market, his reluctant presence would once again be felt and to my surprise and shame, for a fleeting moment I felt again, that sharp pang of guilt. Shrugging it off and satisfied with the dress rehearsal, I had lowered the blind for the final time ahead of her West end debut.

The game of Monopoly, turned Snakes and Ladders, was it had seemed, destined to end in a good old-fashioned game of Chess. I had made my move, deploying his most iconic and celebrated endeavour as an unwilling pawn in my game.

Boarding a flight bound for LAX the following morning and with the game now firmly in play, I had decided to make myself purposefully and provocatively scarce. I had known that installing the work in Mayfair was a last 'make or break' gesture, a gamble that had the potential to save Bankrobber or destroy it. A cunning and calculated act of bravado or a fool's errand. Past experience had prepared me for the vociferous outpouring of rage that my actions would induce, first through Pest Control's haughty admonishments, then at the hands of an impotent army of cyber-warriors stabbing feverishly at their keyboards and lastly by a fawning bunch of left-leaning journalists who railed against Bankrobber's every action in the vain hope that they might curry favour with the great man. Nothing had prepared me for what came next.

On touching down in California I had been met with the grim news that, back in London, there had been no rage or rancour, just an orderly and polite cluster of enthusiastic selfie-seeking tourists enjoying the opportunity afforded them, a two-tonne, four-thousand pound a month dud. The red balloon turned lead balloon. A solitary pawn on an empty board.

Ironic then, that it was to be a handshake some five thousand miles away, in the Bay area of San Francisco that had rescued Bankrobber's fortunes.

At the VIP opening of 'Art Silicon Valley' an unassuming Columbo-like character had entered the Keszler Gallery booth, drawn in by its proud display of Banksy street works.

Stephan, its guileful proprietor, sensing he had hooked a big fish (and undeterred by the individual's disheveled appearance) had proceeded to gently reel him in. With the bait taken and the hook having held firm, the movie mogul and my mentor (and friend) agreed on a handsome six-figure sum. And in doing so, had secured the work a one way ticket out of Mayfair, bound for the bright lights of Hollywood.

On the morning of her dispatch a small team of efficient impossibly well-groomed art handlers armed with the kind of equipment one might expect on the set of a Mission Impossible movie had swept into the market with an array of high-tech kit, including a brace of carbon fibre dollys, a featherweight gantry capable of harnessing huge loads and a smartly liveried HIAB crane. In sharp contrast to the 'Laurel and Hardy' farce that had marked her arrival to the market, her exit had been like watching an excerpt from Nureyev's Swan Lake, a flawless practiced and polished performance.

Witnessing her disappear down White Horse Street and lowering the blind for perhaps the last time, I had felt an overwhelming sense of relief. Through no real play on my part, the gamble had paid off. I had been saved by the remote philanthropic musings of a movie mogul, whose career had spanned several decades and charmed a generation with its tales of derring-do and intergalactic strife.

With my own epic adventure bought to a satisfactory close, I had sat at my customary velvet-lined booth at Mayfair's 'Little House'. Looking up, I had been met by the pained and world-weary gaze of Harrison Ford's Han Solo, his leg awkwardly extended in an elaborate splint.

In salute to the thrill and thrall of happenstance I had raised a glass "May the Force be with you"…

[GIRL WITH BALOON] Stencil & Spray Paint on render and brick - Sold.

KARMA POLICE

KARMA POLICE

There exists an apocryphal tale, that in the public foyer of Cheltenham's GCHQ (Government Communications Headquarters - Britain's global surveillance centre) there hangs a framed print of the Banksy artwork known as 'Spy Booth' underneath which it proudly proclaims in bold letters...

IT'S WHAT WE DO...

It's April 2014, the call had come through that a Banksy mural had appeared on the gable-end wall of a residential house, just three miles east of the controversial GCHQ listening centre. The mural featured three trench-coated, sunglass-sporting 'Spooks' huddled around a public phone box, holding various analogue listening devices. It was generally presumed to stand as a critique by the artist on the controversial practice of covertly harvesting mass surveillance.

I am strapped firmly into the passenger seat of my fixer Sky Grimes 'Black on Black' carbon edition Ferrari 458 Italia, powered by a 4,499 cc V8 engine that threatened to deliver a disconcerting 570 Horsepower. We were due to meet the owner of the freshly adorned property, the assumed beneficiary of Banksy's latest sortie, at a discreetly off-grid country pub some five miles outside the spa town of Cheltenham. With good reason the owner of the house was nervous about drawing unwarranted attention and understandably mistrustful of our motives. He was concerned that our involvement could be seen as provocative in the eyes of the local press who were already busy celebrating the surprise arrival of this new trophy to their town. As we broke free from the residential constraints of Shepherd's Bush and hurtled at breakneck speed onto the M40, it had dawned on me with a modicum of concern, that I had actually never seen Sky outside of the confines of his West London manor. The extraordinary force of nature that defined his character, was, I realised, tamed to my eyes by our shared experience.

I had first come across him when managing a small gallery just off West London's iconic Portobello Road. He had walked-in and brazenly put a pound coin down against a large and very expensive artwork featuring an arrest-shot of the Sex Pistols bassist Sid Vicious. I'd assumed he was another time-waster who was unlikely to return. But good to his word, the very next afternoon he had trucked up with an envelope of cash to complete the purchase, only to then aggressively demand back his pound coin from the previous day. I had learnt early on in our relationship that trying to read Sky's mood was an entirely futile exercise. To suggest he put the 'bi' in bipolar would not be an exaggeration. However what I had learned over the ensuing years is that he was never less than entertaining and most importantly, always got things done. Now, charging at ever more alarming speed into the unfamiliar countryside, it had struck me for the first time that we might indeed look more than a little out of place in the rural idyll of our proposed destination.

Not wanting to draw unnecessary attention, we had edged quietly into the pub's car park with the engine switched to stealth mode. But for all our effort, we might as well have climbed out of a flying saucer wearing silver suits and brandishing ray-guns for the obvious alarm and scrutiny our arrival had invited. Settling at a corner table in the pub's lounge we waited as the locals grudgingly resumed their daily routine. Some forty minutes later an all-black Bentley Continental Sport pulled up outside. At its wheel a young black man could be seen nervously rehearsing his role in the impending drama. I had sensed that this second uninvited intrusion of the morning was almost more than the pub's all-white audience could bear. Anxiously, they had watched on as he stepped out of his car with its deep-tinted windows and sumptuous brothel-red leather interior, taking a moment to check both his watch and reflection before entering the pub's lounge. Sauntering arrogantly over to where we were sat, he had placed the Bentley key fob purposefully and deliberately on the table before him. This tiny ill-judged act had set the tone for the remainder of the meeting. Sky set about dressing him down with a remorseless onslaught of gibes and taunts. Finally, with the balance of power restored, the deflated target of Sky's ire had gone on to explain that he was the shared owner of the Cheltenham property, that it was a rental that had lain empty since an unspecified violent incident had occurred within its walls and that its tenants had fled into the night on the arrival of members of the local constabulary.

Satisfied with our credentials, clearly encouraged by examples of our past successes and with dollar signs burning fiercely in his eyes, he had agreed to take us to the site of his newly acquired spoils. His swagger on leaving the pub, only imperceptibly dented at the sight of our gleaming black stallion, its engine still steaming from the mornings exertions, like a Gold Cup champion in the winner's enclosure.

Having entered the address details into the Satnav, Sky had casually challenged him to "keep up". To anyone within earshot it might have read as a bit of playful banter but I had registered a worrying change in Sky's demeanour. Far from being an idle jest, this had clearly been a gauntlet thrown down, his way of reprimanding his hapless victim for having arrived late to our meeting. Whilst Zero to 60mph in 3.2 seconds seemed on paper quite feasible, within the confines of a crowded pub car park it had proved manifestly and clinically insane. The roar of the V8, 570 horsepower engine, turned into a scream as we hit the tarmac, leaving a vortex of dust and gravel in our wake. As our speed had increased, it seemed that the road's width had decreased incrementally. The calm impassive voice of the Satnav was sending us ever deeper into the heart of the Gloucestershire countryside. Suddenly and without warning, the tarmac track we had been racing down had become not only frighteningly narrow, bordered as it was on both sides by dark vertiginously threatening hedgerows, but had now developed an alarming and resplendent mohawk of grass to its centre, which suddenly and without warning dwindled into little more than a one-horse bridleway. Punctuated by a brutal series of cattle grids that tore ferociously at the underbelly of our chariot, the remaining few hundred yards of the journey had been achieved through sheer inertia and momentum rather than any result of traction to surface. We were effectively sliding recklessly at one hundred miles per hour in a £200k 'Black on Black' Italian sled, one that had, violently and without warning, emptied itself unapologetically onto an urban back-street, unruffled and remarkably intact. To his credit our pursuer had proved himself game to the challenge and had kept up throughout. But, as a young man of colour, when he stepped out of his car on that late spring afternoon, he had appeared every bit as white as Cheltenham could have wished for.

A small crowd of suspicious and hostile onlookers had borne witness to our incongruous arrival on that first day, followed within minutes, by a number of Cheltenham constabulary's finest, their flashing lights and sirens further shattering the afternoon calm. They were clearly relishing the urgency of the unfolding drama and uncertain as to whose side they should be taking, they had erred on the side of caution and quite correctly gone with the guys with the expensive cars, immediately throwing a protective cordon around us and our vehicles. Following the now-familiar exchange of business cards and credentials and a series of bizarre photo-ops which saw each officer sitting enthusiastically behind the wheel of our Ferrari, they had set about dispersing the increasingly agitated and aggressive group and for the remainder of that afternoon had stood guard, their radios crackling with confused and contradictory commands as passing drivers hurled sporadic insults. During this time we were given a tour of the gloomy and neglected interior of the ironically named 159 Fairview Road, an unremarkable end of terrace house, which reeked of poverty and penury. From the off, it had troubled me that this seemed a particularly random choice of canvas for this the artist's most recent missive and I remained sceptical. Something felt wrong with the building's choice and even the centrepiece of the mural (a tatty aluminium framed 1980's KX100 telephone kiosk) had seemed at odds with the artist's familiar signature motifs. Unusually it would be a further 58 days before Banksy would lay claim to the work's authorship in a seemingly random Q&A on his website... and a further eight months before it struck me, that when it came to Banksy there was no such thing as random.

On confirming that the mural, now known locally as 'Spy Booth', was indeed that of the elusive artist, things began to get interesting. Factions and friendships were formed, the denizens of a nearby pub became the enthusiastic guardians of the work, zealously chasing off would-be vandals and thieves, and for the price of a round of drinks would gleefully regale enquiring journalists with spurious tales of late nighttime sightings of the artist. The chair of the local 'Women's Business Club' had set out her stall as being the front runner to protect this, now much cherished, landmark. She had been joined by a self-styled 'millionaire philanthropist' of dubious pedigree who together, in a not entirely convincing act of altruism, had committed to raising sufficient funds to purchase both the painting and the property "in order for it to be held and protected in perpetuity for the enjoyment of the local community and its widening global audience".

Conversely the shared freeholder, a publicity shy individual who had been dragged reluctantly into the fray by a local investigative journalist, had been all too happy to wash his hands of all responsibility regarding the mural, allowing free reign to Sky and his new partner in crime, the hapless cohort whom he had previously taunted so cruelly. They had now inexplicably bonded and together had been busily hatching an elaborate plot to remove the exterior flank wall, with its adorned surface from within the very house itself.

I had chosen to step away from the whole debacle, confident there was little chance of finding an equitable resolution to this particular painting's fate. I opted instead to focus on my newly opened Bankrobber space in Mayfair's Shepherd Market. I did however receive regular Saturday morning updates. Having purchased his cigars from the local smoke shop, Sky would come by to regale me with tales of their Colditz-style antics. He had carefully hand-picked a team of burly and stoic Eastern European scaffolders who, each night as darkness fell, were smuggled into the property and would, without the use of power tools, toil through the night. Leaving each dawn, carrying sacks filled with rubble.

The plan, I was assured, was a "no-brainer". A supporting steel joist had been put in place to avoid the building's collapse and once the internal wall had been sufficiently dismantled and the final brick skin reached, it would be a simple case of attaching a plywood backboard, followed by four neat cuts and... job done!

It was to enable those four simple cuts, that an eight-foot hoarding had been hurriedly constructed which ran the length of the building with an access panel to one end, giving just sufficient space for one of his team to access with a diamond-bladed circular saw. This sudden and unexpected construction had caused a ripple of concern amongst locals who, quite correctly, had suspected foul play. Local reporters, sensing that the game was in play, had plagued me with questions and speculation had abounded that its removal was imminent. An aggrieved band of local protesters including children had staged a nightly candlelit vigil to protect the work from possible removal. Television crews set up camp in the nearby streets and journalists paced anxiously in anticipation of the impending heist.

But in the end it wasn't Sky's madcap plan that was to sound the death knell for Cheltenham's 'Spy Booth' but instead a wild card, a joker in the pack that no one could possibly have anticipated. So it was, that in a bizarre turn of events, a retired local surveyor had taken interest in the case and, as a result of many hours of rigorous research, had uncovered documentation that appeared to assert that the external flank wall of 159 Fairview Road had in fact been the internal wall of a long since demolished property, the victim of a compulsory purchase order made by a local government department in the late 1960's to facilitate a road-widening scheme.

It pointed to the fact, that the true legal ownership of the adorned wall now lay with the department of transport. Excitedly seizing on this newfound knowledge, the local council, urgently (and successfully) petitioned to implement a retrospective planning order, which was duly granted in the February of 2015 effectively (and somewhat remarkably) giving the Banksy artwork, 'Grade II' listed status.

It had been almost a year since we had first visited the site of the now much celebrated mural. Back then, we had ridden into town on the back of a 570 Horsepower promise, wearing our customary black hats, armed only with the intention to profit from the sale of what I considered to be a rather ugly and difficult work. But in the light of its newly-bestowed status, I had decided on a strategic change of tack, rather than being the perennial bad guys we would instead be sporting the white hats on this occasion. Like the Lone Ranger and Tonto, bravely and selflessly supporting the rescue of this much lauded masterpiece. Naming and shaming the pariahs who had sought to make profit from the messianic daubing's of the genius that was Banksy.

Perplexed by this sudden about-turn, the press were forced, in public at least, to grudgingly applaud this newly adopted stance. There followed a number of lazy, halfhearted attempts to raise funds to purchase the property. There had even been fanciful talk of creating a Banksy museum in the house, or of turning it into a holiday destination. But it quickly became apparent, that all anyone in Cheltenham had really ever sought from Banksy's gift was self-aggrandisement. There had been no real appetite to invest from any legitimate parties and the ill-judged 'Cease and Desist' order had ironically left the work hopelessly vulnerable. A spokesman for the Gloucestershire Police department put out a press statement that there had been an increased presence of officers in the area as a result of "building social tension" which had developed among residents who feared for the work's future.

Spy booth was attacked three times over the ensuing months. The first had resulted in the spooks faces being drunkenly and clumsily whited out, only to be saved by locals before the paint had the chance to dry. The second, a more concerted and vicious effort utilising silver and red spray-paint maliciously applied to the render's surface, all but obscuring the work. But fatally, it was the third attack which had proved to be the coup de grâce, dealt at the hands of 'Jack Frost'. The silent assassin had crept insidiously into the neglected fabric of the building, bringing the mural to its knees and collapsing it, leaving little more than a pile of rubble. A sad and sallow end, to a chapter that had never really delivered on its promise to any one party and had once again exposed the hollow profanity of greed.

The Banksy artwork had attracted thousands of visitors from all over the UK and abroad since its first appearance on 13th April 2014. Two years later, in early 2016, the property owner, having been so vilified in the press (to the point that he had been the victim of a number of anonymous death threats) finally put the property up for sale through local Estate Agents Peter Ball & Co, with a guide price of two hundred and ten thousand pounds.

Karma Police (usually capitalised as KARMA POLICE) was the code name given for an Internet mass surveillance and data collection programme operated by the United Kingdom's Government Communications Headquarters (GCHQ) based on the outskirts of Cheltenham Spa. A programme that had played an important part in exposing the whistle blower Edward Snowden. Supposedly named after the Radiohead song 'Karma Police' which had included in its lyric "This is what you'll get when you mess with us."

Q

Q

Lift Scaffolding Limited, was incorporated in the April of 2006 on the strength of a Coutts bank loan of three hundred thousand pounds, its guarantor the artist Damien Hirst. Danny Moynihan a close friend of Hirst, who in the nineties had shared a pair of apartments in the former New York loft of artist Jasper John, was one of four partners in Lift Scaffolding. Moynihan, a successful art dealer and author of 'Boogie-Woogie' a novel charting the excesses of the eighties art world in New York, had been looking to diversify. Partnering-up with Sky Grimes, had presumably seemed a diversion worth pursuing.

Both Danny and Sky had visited my Lonsdale Road space on a number of occasions toward the end of 2007 but it was a lone visit by Sky that was to spark a fire that would burn brightly for the next decade and beyond.

I had recently acquired a collection of Banksy works that had been hung resplendent against Bankrobber's newly polished bare plaster walls and it was on this visit that, for only the second time in our acquaintance, his attention had been piqued by art. In the first instance by the previous year's purchase of the Sid Vicious Mug Shot (on the occasion of our first meeting) and this time by a small monochrome print featuring a helmet-wearing 'British Bobby', brazenly 'giving the finger' to anyone who glanced his way. Titled 'Rude Copper', the example in question of this, the artist's first print, had been additionally embellished with an aerosol-sprayed silver tag and as a result had carried the not insubstantial price tag of forty five thousand pounds. This second spontaneous reaction in as many years to a piece of art, had clearly caused Sky some consternation. He had mercilessly questioned me as to why he should have to spend such a sum to own this anarchic bauble, during which I had mentioned that the artist Damien Hirst was, himself, a keen collector of this hotly tipped newcomer. This fact had seemed to spark an almost allergic reaction in him and he had abruptly stepped out onto the front deck of Bankrobber to make an urgent and very animated phone call. Aggressively stepping back into the room some minutes later, he confirmed that Hirst was indeed a collector of this elusive new star. Intent on not missing out and in a soon to be familiar show of bravado, Banksy's 'Rude Copper' was sold and a friendship forged.

Sky's right-hand man, Q scaffolding's poetic Zen warrior had once commented with his usual dryly laconic wit that following a visit by the elusive artist, the property owner "might as well start shopping for bricks". This had been his observation on the chain of events that would inevitably follow the discovery of a new Banksy artwork on a building. Firstly the property owner alerted to its arrival would hastily arrange to have security put in place to guard the work from attack. This would usually be followed by the application of a protective Perspex sheet, this had proven to be the best first-line of defence, effectively shielding the work whilst allowing its notoriety to snowball through social media channels and word of mouth. There then followed a nervous wait until the work's authorship would be confirmed by its inclusion on the artist's website in what had now become his established modus operandi. A strangely provocative strategy on the artist's part, effectively throwing down a gauntlet, in the certain knowledge that his offering's perceived value would rocket on being rubber-stamped in such a calculated fashion. A call to arms that would inevitably cause a gold rush of greedy and grasping speculators. Picks and spades at the ready, these avaricious adventurers would clumsily make their moves, only to be confounded by the overwhelming logistics of the task at hand.

Bankrobber, if not the first port of call, had always remained the last. Frustrated freeholders, their dreams of a fast buck extinguished, would reluctantly concede that their only option was to call on our services. Mirroring the Book of Revelation there would then follow four visitations. The first to establish the credentials of the supposed owners and discuss the notional value. The second would take the form of a brief and discreet sortie to assess the viability of the work's removal. The third, a more showy and theatrical ensemble piece that would see us arriving in one of Sky's fleet of blacked-out cars, a strategy aimed at racking up tensions, stirring local unrest and inviting press interest, a carefully orchestrated gambit aimed at building value into the work but one mired in risk, as the level of anger and hostility toward our actions had increased incrementally with each successful removal. The fourth and final visit marked by the arrival of one of Q's lavishly liveried trucks bristling with shiny new scaffolding poles.

Twenty four months after 'Lift Scaffolding's' incorporation, Sky Grimes was unceremoniously ousted from the company in a hostile move based on spurious and wholly unfounded allegations of impropriety. The company limped on for a period but never fully realised its potential. Motivated and energised by anger and revenge, Sky had gone on to create an all-new scaffolding company from the ashes, one whose success can be measured by the prevalence of the vivid green 'Q' logo that dominates the London skyline, rising resplendent and phoenix-like.

Damien Hirst continues to this day to collect and display works by the artist Banksy, no doubt blissfully unaware of the irony attached to that guarantee made more than a decade earlier.

ART BUFF

ART BUFF

Folkestone, fourteen years later and a cordon of police has formed around me. An angry crowd has gathered and a middle-age woman is screaming to anyone who is listening "He's not from around here, look at his shoes, they're not from Primark!!"

This assertion was not inaccurate. The day was set to be the first of a three-day endeavour to remove a Banksy artwork named on the artist's website as 'Art Buff' featuring a pensioner wearing headphones, staring at an empty plinth; presumably as a wry comment on the nature of contemporary art and more particularly, the current crop of community art that littered the streets, parks and beaches of the town's 2014 Triennial celebrations. Folkestone, once a jewel in the crown of Kent's Gold Coast had, over recent years, become a neglected dumping ground for the down-at-heel and dispossessed of the county.

It was the sale of the town's most important employer Saga, a hugely successful local insurance group built by the late Sidney De Haan, that had made a billionaire of his son, the tycoon and philanthropist Sir Roger De Haan.

Sir Roger, had plans for this town and had organised (and funded) an impressive team in the shape of the Creative Foundation whom he had tasked with mining a rich new seam of artistic endeavour. Part of this had involved purchasing great swathes of the town's commercial real estate and making it affordably available to carefully chosen creative projects. His unflinching ambition to restore the fortunes of this broken down South Coast 'Coney Island' knew no bounds, a Xanadu to his Kubla Khan. In doing so, he had unwittingly pitted himself against my will, setting in motion a very different saga, to that which he was familiar. An epic saga spanning two continents and one that would test judicial practice to its limit and deliver me to the steps of the country's highest court. Kind of.

And so it was, under the light of a waxing crescent moon, midway through Folkestone's Triennial, that an uninvited gesture was visited upon this sleepy seaside town. As early morning joggers and dog walkers braved that September morning, a small crowd had gathered in front of the back wall of one of the town's last surviving amusement arcades, facing blankly onto Payers Park with its back turned to its audience, the pensioner stood stock still in contemplation. A ripple of excitement spread through the town as the artist's website confirmed the work to be by Banksy, provocatively stating it to be "Part Of The Folkestone Triennial. Kind of".

The addition of this new work to the artist's canon had reached me later that morning and I had lazily brushed it of off as being a clumsy imitation of the artist's oeuvre, but just two hours later I was gunning down the M20 in the Bankrobber-mobile, having accepted the invitation from the arcade's owners to advise on its removal and possible sale.

In an insalubrious cafe adjacent to the arcade, negotiations were put in place and a hasty deal was agreed upon. The arcade's owners would cover the not insubstantial cost of physically cutting out the section of wall that the mural had been applied and the further cost of reducing its thickness and preparing the work for sale. In return I would oversee its removal, restoration and eventual sale with the proceeds going to the Jim Godden Memorial Trust. Just as quickly, that same ripple of excitement had reached the desk of the director of the town's Creative Foundation Alastair Upton. Immediately and with steely determination, he had set about laying claim to the work on behalf of its townsfolk, adopting it as a cornerstone to the town's Triennial.

The arcade owners, with similar tenacity, had posted a cartoonishly inappropriate sentry to stand guard over the work whilst its fate was being decided. Very quickly it became apparent that this was a town divided. The new-guard made up of artistically inclined well-meaning folk, supported by the philanthropic De Haan, pitted against the old-guard, who's figurehead, the now deceased Jimmy Godden, a colourful amusement-arcade tycoon and serial entrepreneur who had in an homage to Brooklyn's coastal resort created his own 'Playground of the World' in the shape of the town's beachfront Rotunda and Funfair - sadly now vanished in a reckless and misguided early attempt at regeneration.

It was time to take sides and I had been charmed by the Godden family mythology and the slightest ghost of a memory that I had visited and enjoyed their pastiche of a playground in my youth. In contrast, I didn't like what I saw as being a smug sense of entitlement, which accompanied the actions of the town's self-appointed benefactor. I also didn't like the assumption and (to my mind) misplaced assertion that this artwork was delivered as anything other than a sarcastic rebuke toward the empty gesture-politics of community art, rather than being a generous attempt by the artist to be included in the town's bloated and overblown pageant.

Having chosen my side, I set about putting together a firm capable of carrying out what was clearly going to be an unpopular and audacious heist. To take the heat out of the situation and in the spirit of compromise I had agreed to delaying the removal until after the Triennial's close. This was an expensive strategy and one that would require the work to be protected 24/7 by a private security team paid for by the Godden family. Over the following weeks a hilarious 'changing of the guard' ritual developed. A scruffy charabang of chain smoking security staff bore bemused witness to a tide of admirers who had come from all over the country and beyond to pay pilgrimage to the shrine that was 'Art Buff'. I would sit for hours watching these pilgrims with their unbowed enthusiasm. Minibuses would deliver enthusiastic wedding parties.

Stags and hens drunkenly posed with its impassive central character. From dawn till dusk, a generationally democratic tide of onlookers would file through Payers Park to pay their respects.

The pleasure and attention this humble artwork was attracting was beginning to haunt and concern me. Daily, I would receive scornful glances of disgust and contempt as people began to join the dots. Stories abounded about my nefarious presence and intention and I had taken to ensuring I had company on my visits. Additionally, a cottage industry had sprung up around the work, tote bags and T-Shirts, guided tours and discussions were making it and the town, famous. But it was behind closed doors in an office somewhere within the creative foundation's headquarters, less than a quarter of a mile away, that a more powerful and sinister plot was being hatched in an attempt to foil my plans.

It's the morning of the 3rd November, two days before my fifty-sixth birthday. I'm on site at Payers Park. Alongside me, my seasoned fixer, Sky Grimes and his team of foot soldiers were taking final instruction. It had been decided that we would need to drill through the back of the wall accessed through the arcade's laughably named 'Secure Room' - a windowless, cluttered and chaotic counting house, sporting little more than a kettle and a number of pushed-together Formica tables piled high with coins. In one corner, a vastly out of scale cast iron safe sitting precisely where we were required to drill. I was instantly reminded of the scene from 'The Italian Job' in which its central protagonist, Charlie Croker drily commented, "You're only supposed to blow the bloody doors off" as scorched banknotes rained down around him.

It was clear this was not going to be the polished operation we had planned. Two hours later and the drilling had begun, the 16inch-long diamond-tipped drill bit screamed angrily as the render and concrete resisted its unwarranted incursion. As the counting room filled with choking black dust, I stepped out into the bright light of the morning to discover that the drilling had acted as a call to arms. An increasingly hostile crowd had gathered, some with their ears pressed firmly to the wall. I realised we had grossly underestimated the passion invoked by the work's threatened removal, and by the end of that first day as my team progressed to the outside flank of the wall, it became obvious they were not going to let this progress without protest. Worst still, the alarm had now reached my newly anointed nemesis Alastair Upton, who had called on the services of the local constabulary to halt our progress.

In an unexpected and bizarre twist of fate, the dozen or so police officers who attended and assessed the scene that afternoon made the measured and extraordinary decision that, it was in fact we, who were at risk from the baying mob and promptly threw a protective cordon around us as we continued noisily on with our task.

The woman hadn't been wrong. The shoes I had chosen for that day's theatre were a handsome pair of blue metal-studded, hand-built Church's 'Shanghai Brogues' fashioned from a vintage 'last', not used since the shoe was first launched in 1929 on the eve of the Great Depression, when the Stock Market lost almost 90 percent of its value, signalling the longest and most severe economic downturn in modern history.

MIAMI VICE

MIAMI VICE

The Christmas lights swayed violently in the wake of a Miami squall, the lavishly adorned palm trees furiously trying to shake off their wildly inappropriate seasonal adornments. It's December 2014 and I'm looking out over the Miami skyline from a window on the twelfth floor of the fashionable and wildly expensive Delano Hotel. I'm here to chaperone the newly restored 'Art Buff' to its grand unveiling at this year's 'Art Miami' launch party, a lavish and much anticipated annual extravaganza, now entering its 25th year.

Miami had confused me.

Initially I had fallen in love with its fake tan, its veneer of sincerity and Art Deco glamour. But on my second visit, I recognised a darker, more vulgar aspect to its character. It quickly became apparent that pricing wasn't restricted to the art. Everything and everyone here had a price. People would rush between parties like Victorian debutantes greedily marking their dance cards. It wasn't the party you were at, it was the party you were going to that mattered. For five days each December, a cattle market of dealers, hookers and hustlers entered through the doors of these esteemed pleasure palaces moving seamlessly through the lavish foyers, negotiating their way past ever more stringent layers of security, until on the delivery of a neatly folded $100 dollar bill you would be ushered with theatrical ceremony through to the decks and terraces that paid host to the VIP parties and then, after downing a brace of toxically potent cocktails, spilling out onto the immaculately manicured sandy strip of South Beach, pausing only momentarily to wonder in awe at the impossible beauty of the Atlantic Ocean, then swiftly on to the next party. A drunken, enthusiastic tide that ebbed and flowed, through the packed corridors and lounges squeezed between Collins Avenue and the eponymous South Beach.

Whilst the chaos and mayhem of the much-publicised Folkestone removal less than a month earlier had gained us considerable notoriety and extraordinary press coverage, it had struck me that we hadn't made any friends in those closing weeks of October and even now as I stood admiring the glow that emanated from the neon signs of the surrounding hotels, it further struck me that we might indeed have made at least one formidable enemy.

Rumours had reached me that back in England a last-minute legal case was, even now at the eleventh hour, being petitioned to stop the sale of 'Art Buff'. But as I walked the length of the Delano's absurdly opulent Philippe Starck-designed lobby, that all seemed very distant and unlikely. The central argument, I was told was that by our removing the work from its original site we had in some fashion infringed the artist's intellectual rights. I had successfully challenged this assertion on a number of previous occasions and would certainly not be backing down on this one. Many thousands of pounds had been invested in this project, from its removal to an extensive schedule of repair and restoration and finally an eye-wateringly expensive last-minute flight to ensure it would arrive in time for tomorrow's star-studded event.

Dressed in a provocatively antagonistic (yet hopelessly inappropriate) Richard James bespoke camouflaged suit, my confidence buoyed by one too many margaritas and a misplaced sense of self, I stepped out of the Delano's air-conditioned lobby into the Florida night and was immediately hit by an unforgiving wall of humidity. By the time I was delivered onto the fair's red carpet, I was soaked to my skin and my earlier confidence had been replaced by a now all too familiar sense of unease. Had anything really changed since my first East Coast debacle seven years earlier? Yes, the stakes were considerably higher this time around as was the potential reward. But the one thing that had not changed was the fact that we were flying in the face of the artist's wishes.

Like the British archaeologist Howard Carter and his sponsor Lord Carnarvon before us, I was beginning to worry we would be exposed as little more than latter-day grave robbers and that our Banksy trophies, like the contents of Tutankhamun's tomb, would carry with them their own curse.

Over the next five days an estimated 82,500 art tourists filed past Banksy's recalcitrant art critic.

Pest Control issued a statement, "We have warned Mr. Keszler and Mr. Barton of the serious implications of selling unauthenticated works but they seem to not care. We have no doubt that these works will come back to haunt them both."

DREAMLAND

DREAMLAND

The Folkestone Creative Foundation, in response to the public backlash against the work's removal, began legal proceedings with the aim of securing the return of the Banksy to Folkestone. The first step was to obtain an injunction preventing Dreamland, and those involved with it, from selling or having further dealings with the Banksy.

Due diligence. Two words that certainly were set to haunt me. But as I mounted the steps to No.29 York Street, an unremarkable town house in London's Marylebone, on this fine spring morning, I am in fighting spirits.

It had been four months since my return from Miami and I had satisfied myself that the barrage of negative publicity that had followed the removal of 'Art Buff' and its subsequent turbulent transatlantic journey, had been directly responsible for its failure to find a buyer and I was here to redress the balance. As I entered the offices of 'Brook Martin & Co Solicitors' I felt like a man on a mission. Michael Maurice Martin was to be our gladiator in this fight, a suave reassuring blend of John Thaw's 'Morse' and Martin Shaw's 'Judge John Deed' with a comfortable, confident countenance. Pitched against the colder more calculated Tim Maxwell of Boodle Hatfield LLC who carried with him the air of a poker player carrying a knowingly winning hand.

The scene had been set. It was to be 'Dreamland Leisure Limited vs The Creative Foundation' a David and Goliath affair but one I fully intended to play my part in winning. I had extensively researched my subject and had become something of an expert in intellectual copyright law and although I wasn't a plaintiff in the case, I was cited as an expert witness, which gave me the benefit of being centre stage whilst not being financially liable. I was relishing the prospect of having my day in court and not just any court, the highest court of the land, The High Court.

I spent the evenings of that spring, drinking cheap white wine and rehearsing my role, one I had been working toward for more than eight years. I would take to the stand preening and posturing like a preposterous, parody Perry Mason, in my newly built Black Watch tartan three-piece and would clearly and confidently assert my case, one whose central tenet lay at the very heart of my argument: That Banksy's celebrated and much admired daubings amounted to little more than illegal uninvited acts of vandalism and, as such, their author had no legal redress or claim to ownership, intellectually or otherwise. Job done, take a bow and exit stage right to awed silence, followed by wild applause.

It's April 1st, 2015 April Fools' Day. I'm sitting in the wood-panelled basement of Bankrobber's Mayfair headquarters, staring at a white A5 envelope that had inauspiciously arrived in that morning's post, an envelope bearing the sinister sender address of 'Boodle Hatfield LLP'. I had previously been made aware, that this esteemed law firm had been elected to play the role of Goliath against our David. But that they had deigned to contact me directly was unsettling in the extreme. It would be a further two hours before I summoned the courage to open and unfold the contents of this unwelcome auger of doom.

Claim No: HC-2015-001297 a red stamped 'Order for an injunction' made for an uncomfortable read. Penal notice 2. Until further order:
b. Without prejudice to generality of the foregoing, the Respondents must instruct Mr. Stephan Keszler, the Keszler Gallery, New York Mr. Robin Barton and the Bankrobber Gallery not to sell, transfer, move, dispose of, damage, deface or otherwise deal with the mural

known as "Art Buff". Any breach of which may result in being held to be in contempt of court and may be imprisoned, fined or have their assets seized.

With only days to go, my much anticipated debut had been cruelly snatched from my grasp. The stage lights abruptly dimmed, the set broken down, the theatre dark. There was to be no awed silence or wild applause, no redemptive and glorious after-party. My day in court had been indefinitely cancelled, replaced instead by a horrible and cold realisation that the whole sad and sorry saga of 'Art Buff' with its 8,968 mile transatlantic round-trip, legal largesse and many thousands of pounds of investment had failed. Not on some newly born legal milestone, or hard fought redefining of intellectual copyright law, but on a stupid character flaw on my part, one in which I had allowed my heart to rule my head. My love of the underdog had, not for the first time, clouded my judgement. Eight months earlier to the day when I had sat in that insalubrious Folkestone cafe adjacent to that now-notorious arcade, broken bread with the materfamilias Rochelle Godden and her two sons Jeremy and Jordan, I had neglected to ask one simple question.

...

Two years later, the morning of the 7th May 2017, a representative for the elusive artist confirmed that a vast Brexit-inspired mural applied to the gable-end wall of Castle Amusements sited in the coastal port of Dover, depicting a workman atop a ladder chipping away at one of the twelve stars of the European flag, was indeed the work of Banksy.

The legal and confirmed freeholder of Castle Amusements 'Company Number 03114067 Dreamland Leisure Limited - principal director: James 'Jimmy' Godden.

COMPLIANCE

COMPLIANCE

It had been 8,395 days since the hammer had come down on Lot no.33 Pablo Picasso's Women of Algiers [Version 0] making a record $31.9m in front of an enthusiastic audience of some 2,000 people. Countless records had since been set, a seemingly tireless ascent reaching ever higher peaks. Andy Warhol's 'Triple Elvis' $81.9m, Francis Bacon's 'Triptych,1976' $86.3m, Edvard Munch's 'The Scream' $119.9m, Gustav Klimt's 'Woman in Gold' $135m, but most astonishingly and perplexing, Leonardo da Vinci's 'Salvator Mundi' had fetched an unprecedented world record price of $450.3m. The very same painting had been sold through Sotheby's in 1958 for the princely sum of £45. Meaning that in the span of my lifetime, this dubiously attributed bauble of High Renaissance heritage, measuring just eighteen by twenty-six inches, had accrued an added annual value of $6.5m dollars for each year of my life.

At some point over those 23 years, a veiled mist-thin madness had crept into the auction houses and galleries. A puffery and arrogance had taken hold, a collective amnesia to any sense of truth or reality. The bubble that had looked certain to burst after the banking crisis of 2008 had instead continued to grow exponentially and at an accelerated almost grotesque rate. At Christie's New York, in an ironic but largely overlooked display of vacuity, a Jeff Koons Rabbit - a giant, highly polished, gaudy reimagining of an inflatable children's toy, had fetched a record $91.1m to rapturous applause, marking it out as the most expensive artwork ever sold by a living artist. The party just kept rolling on, auction houses were overwhelmed by crowds eager to be part of the spectacle.

Auctioneers had acquired rock star status, ambition and greed writ large. But as the year had progressed, there were mutterings and murmurings in the wings. The stratospheric headline-stealing results, whilst reassuringly robust to the industry, were now attracting the attention of previously disinterested parties. It had long been suspected that the art trade's oblique nature had made it a perfect bedfellow to the nefarious workings and machinations of unscrupulous money launderers. But with the evidence provided within the leaked Panama Papers, questions now abounded regarding the veracity of many of the reported acquisitions and their murky acquirers. Extraordinary deals had been exposed as being, at the very least, shady and at worst, criminal. Sinisterly named shell companies propped up by offshore accounts of dubious tenure, located in obscure jurisdictions and territories across the globe (Panama City, Belize, Cayman Islands and The British Virgin Islands) had all paid host to, and expressed scant regard for, either their legitimacy or authority. There had long been in place a tacit understanding that, unlike property and shares, there existed no central register to the ownership of art, or indeed any mandatory regulation, making it a uniquely versatile market, but one inherently susceptible and vulnerable to abuse. Those few regulations that were in place had remained largely unchecked and unchanged for generations, practiced and policed by a close-knit community of dealers and collectors, whose value of good manners, trust and fair play bore echoes to their Victorian forbears. Historically the vast majority of private sales had been carried out behind closed doors, often sealed with little more than a handshake. Even the apparent public-facing of the major auction houses, deliberately disguised the fact that although the sale prices were made a matter of public record, there remained no obligation or appetite to disclose either the identity of the seller nor buyer.

But the financial regulators had smelled blood and as the art market gnawed feverishly at the trapped torpid limb of its excesses in a futile attempt to free itself from this unwarranted scrutiny, the authorities had closed in for the kill. The cloak of secrecy that had shrouded the industry's murky waters for so many decades had been lifted and its opaque and secretive nature exposed. The Panamanian rock located at the Pacific entrance to the notorious canal had been upturned to expose an infestation of dark dealings, subterfuge and criminality. The leaked papers had exposed the enormity and extent of the money launderers' activities that had for so long been overlooked, hiding in plain sight. Initially the regulators' questions had been met with mild distain but this had rapidly turned to panic as the poured-over papers had brought to light a litany of the great and the good of the art world. All implicated by association to a vast complex web of deceit and evasion.

In response to the tightening regulatory net, the old-school art-world habitués had closed ranks, circled their wagons and retreated to the safe havens of their private clubs and closeted rooms to weather it out. Yes they had lost control of the reins for now but they had remained stoic, consoling themselves in the knowledge that their trade had survived many such storms over its one-hundred-and-forty-year lifetime since first setting up stall at its New Bond Street headquarters in 1876.

In a bold and determined attempt to effect a coup d'etat, the EU regulationary committee had passed a declaration; as from January 2020 a new edict would be mandated. The Fifth Anti-Money Laundering Directive [COMPLIANCE] was an EU Initiative which had set in law, that any art transaction worth more than €10,000 euros demanded that the seller be legally bound to provide extensive personal details of the buyer, including their address and passport details. Even the most complex web of umbrella and shell companies uncovered in the leaked Panama Papers were to be bought to heal by this draconian order, demanding that by whatever evidential proofs necessary, the identity of the [ultimate beneficial owner] must also be declared.

In contrast to the old-school's reaction, the brazen new pariahs were enjoying their newfound status and were not about to relinquish or let go of their new toy without a fight. Swiftly re-evaluating the new landscape and in a nimble attempt to shake off their pursuers, they had adopted ever more complex methods of transaction. The most divisive being the employment of [Freeports] vast anonymous, climate controlled tax-haven storage units sited outside of the reach of the European Union, trading floors where art could be stored indefinitely and bought and sold without even leaving the facility. These ultra-secure, tardis-like cathedrals, had evolved from dusty grain warehouses, where weights and measures had been exacted into state-of-the-art architectural monoliths, comprising private viewing suites and 24 hour armed security. Sited within limousine-reach of private airfields, these new high-tech trading hubs were the perfect foil to the regulators probing questions. The most impressive being Singapore's 'Le Freeport' a standalone oasis of calm, an architecturally honed facility, scrupulously styled to a standard that would make any Bond Villain proud, and at its heart a vast, mirror-finished steel sculptural work by the superstar designer Ron Arad ironically titled 'La Cage sans Frontieres' [Cage without borders].

The irony being that these buildings were precisely that, a cage, albeit a gilded one. Great and important artworks were being delivered with unnerving regularity to these sinister silos where they would be evaluated, logged, polished and preened in preparation to being paraded before the steely gaze of the ultra-wealthy. Doomed to become pawns in an endless trade, where huge sums can be leveraged against the perceived value of an artwork without its new owner ever actually seeing it. In a vulgar display of contempt, this new breed of dealers and collectors had seized the old world order from under the sleepy watch of its fusty forebears and re-fashioned it into a cynical reimagining of the very system that had seen them banished into the wilderness just three decades earlier. The jostling arrogant glass edifices of eighties excess, replaced by impenetrable somber trading tombs. Within whose walls, an estimated 80 percent of the world's most important paintings and artworks will remain incarcerated, reduced to little more than a commodity, a trading tool in a world consumed by greed.

In August 2018 'The Fine Art Society' - London's oldest commercial gallery, closed its doors for the last time at its New Bond Street headquarters.

WHEN WE WERE KINGS

WHEN WE WERE KINGS

It is London December 2019. It is the last evening of the decade, one that had promised everything, delivered much but ultimately had been found wanting. Looking out from the first-floor window of my narrow rented Victorian brick-built terraced house, at the north-eastern corner of Mayfair's Shepherd Market, a near-invisible hideaway, situated at the furthest end of White Horse Street, and one which, until recently, had served as a private brothel - a 'Mayfair walk-up'. On one side, the market's last remaining working house, its windows shielded by a clumsily applied voile of red, on the other, a cartoonishly carved depiction of a vine heavy with ripe fruit, the Dionysian talisman of 'The Grapes Tavern' which served as a bacchanalian cornerstone to the market I had made my stage.

It had been five years since the ill-judged fiasco that was 'Stealing Banksy' and I was still feeling the repercussions. The show had ended as it had begun, badly. The final straw having come when, attending the show's wrap party on the hotel's sumptuous roof terrace, the warmth of the evening's golden sunset had been momentarily interrupted by the now familiar approach of Devil, my newly adopted minder. His vast shadow preceding him like an ominous portent.

From our very first meeting, I had enjoyed Devil's ebullient and timely interjections. But on this occasion, his customary unruffled countenance had looked unusually pained and I had correctly sensed this was not to be one of his finest. The news he had brought should not have surprised me but nonetheless it did. What should have marked the somewhat somber end to a rather sordid chapter had been further marred by news that the hotel management were effectively holding the entire collection, including 'No Ball Games' to ransom pending payment of a substantial release-fee, without payment of which, none of the works were to leave the premises. As a consequence, I had been left with the onerous task of telling its owners that their already nebulous investment, had through no fault of their own, become a frozen asset, a hostage to fortune. The owners had trusted in my decision to consign their work to this sad and sorry circus, but with the big top collapsed, the crowds gone and their anonymity compromised, all I could advise is that they meet the ransom and make a dignified retreat.

I had not enjoyed being part of the charade that was 'Stealing Banksy'. The daily lineups had made me uncomfortable, conjuring unwelcome ghosts from the past. The gnawing doubts that had haunted me since the earliest days of Bankrobber had been reignited at the sight of the lines of enthusiastic acolytes, patiently and politely queueing like so many wide-eyed children, their entrance fees pressed firmly into hot sweaty palms, excitedly awaiting access to the promised pantomime. It had again begged the question; what was it that inspired such blind devotion to a person whose likely contempt for them might be matched only by that of mine for him?

There was something in his controlling nature that I had disliked from the start. It was what had set the game in play, been the driving force behind Bankrobber, its raison d'être. From that very first rebuke, I had relished the imprecations and threats. I had become addicted to the adrenalin-fuelled antics, the physical hurdles set ever higher as Banksy had attempted to thwart my endeavours. What started as a dare had become an obsession.

It had now been twelve years since I opened Bankrobber. Intentioned as a defiant gesture against the white-walled iniquities of Mayfair's bloated behemoths, the arrogant and oppressive institutions which had defined the art world for decades past. The sterile galleries with their hermetically-sealed entranceways and haughty demeanour had become lazy, complacent and increasingly impotent. I had sensed that the tide was turning and I was determined to be one of the new model army that was poised to overturn the old order.

But fate had determined that I follow a very different path. Had I not picked up the phone on that dark January evening a decade earlier, how very different things might have been. The blithely-issued threat, "You can't do that," that had served as my call to arms, had spurred me on. Time after time Bankrobber had flown in the face of the artist's wishes, arrogantly ignoring the hexes, revelling in the egregious behaviour and savouring the reprehensible condemnation that had followed my every action.

It had indeed been a glorious decade, one swathed in excess and adventure. Newspaper headlines had cried "Cheat!" Accusations of thievery and foul play had abounded. The services of both Scotland Yard and the FBI had been called upon, questions raised in parliament, councillors lobbied, legal precedents set and broken. It had been a crazed rollercoaster ride littered with first class flights, luxury hotel suites and fast cars. Six letters that had defined a decade, B A N K S Y, a random word that had opened doors to extraordinary places and magnificent events, an 'access all areas' pass to the best parties and the finest clubs. Our reach had known no bounds and our ambition no limits. We had walked like kings, crossed continents, spanned oceans, defied deadlines and denounced doubt, whilst all the while knowing we were on shifting sands.

From our castles on the coast, we had plotted and planned sortie after sortie in an attempt to create and build a market from the errant artist's endeavours only to be outwitted and thwarted at every turn. Whilst our nemesis's anonymity had served him well, it had simultaneously provided a covert platform to my own activities, a splendid near impenetrable smokescreen that obscured and twisted the truth. And although I had never once laid claim to any other title than my own. I had quickly discovered that the more I had renounced the notion of any association or affiliation with the artist the more the notion had stuck. Even my closest friends and acquaintances had succumbed to doubt. If hiding in plain sight had been my intention then I had surely excelled in my goal. The pairing of the words 'Bankrobber' with 'Banksy' had created a bountiful burden, a gift that had kept giving. But then add into the mix, the name 'Robin' and you had a magnificent cocktail, one mired in misinterpretation, a mist-strewn maelstrom of obfuscation. It's true that I could easily have extinguished those early doubts, poured cold water on the rumour and innuendo but instead had willfully chosen to maintain the myth, to gently fan the flames, boastfully basking in their limelight and bizarrely, the more sincere my refutal and the more earnest the delivery the greater the doubt it had imbued.

I had considered myself the master of my own destiny but at some point along the journey things had become blurred and confused. On one occasion, when on being interviewed, my denials, finessed as they were, had been delivered with such clarity and self-belief as to have been received with near incredulity by my inquisitors. So believable and convincing were my protestations that I had even started to accept my own narrative as truth. My very identity had been bought into question, hanging perilously from a thread woven of lies, misrepresentation and mendacity, a masquerade so believable, so entrenched as to seem almost plausible. I had set myself apart from the truth for so long that I had become an imposter in my own life and with the high times now behind me and Bankrobber having been holed below the waterline, its reputation irrevocably damaged, there had felt like nowhere to go.

For so many years I had relied on the actions of another to motivate me and spur me on but with the 'Girl With Balloon' gone and 'No Ball Games' locked in stasis, I had felt my legacy reduced to little more than that of a footnote in someone else's story, my role recused, the script redacted. Perhaps after all we had been, little more than latter-day grave robbers, murky merchants, corrupt carpet-sellers at a filthy souk of our own making, touting our ill-gotten gains in a grubby game of deception. Maybe after all Pest Control's admonishments had come to fruition, their seemingly empty rhetoric and threats, finally realised - and as with

Tutankhamun's curse, we were indeed to be punished for our past improprieties. The victims of our own ill-intentioned greed.

Was it too late to show penitence, to beg forgiveness, atone for our sins, pay reparation for the repeated and unconscionable acts of insolence? I had played a strong hand but one that had changed nothing. I had thought it certain that in time the auction houses and galleries would acquiesce and see sense, but instead they had continued to prostrate themselves at the Messiah's feet in an act of blinkered unquestioning piety. The God of Art had spoken and the art world had listened. The heretics had failed and Bankrobber had become a byword for bad behaviour. Thieves had indeed stolen Banksy's art on many occasions. But I was no thief, just a mischief-maker, an arrogant adventurer that had gone along for the ride, content to act as a thorn in this deity's side. I had felt only mild pangs of conscience along the way and no lasting sense of guilt. There had been no damascene conversion, only the bleak realisation that I had failed in my endeavour. I had played my final hand and lost. I had fought hard to be king but had been exposed as a knave, a charlatan, a one-eyed Jack, a bandit, a blaggard, a bankrobber.

The caller on that evening, a decade earlier, had gone on to ask, "Do you know who I am?"... I hadn't then and I don't now.

I'M GOING TO TEAR YOUR PLAYHOUSE DOWN

I'M GOING TO TEAR YOUR PLAYHOUSE DOWN

[Curtain rises]

Act one: BRISTOL FASHION

Scene 1

[Lights come up on a single figure silhouetted against a rural setting with the London skyline far in the distance]

A long long time ago in the far away land of [Bristolia] a young man had packed together a few meagre possessions, some half-empty spray-cans and some rolls of old stencil paper and had set out to make a name for himself. On settling upon the ancient Gate of [Notting Hill] in the western province of Londinium he began to focus on his practice. His ambition was boundless and he soon began to decorate the streets of his neighbourhood with his playful and subversive daubings, honing his skills and perfecting his craft. Very quickly people began to take notice of the young man's motifs and messages that had begun to adorn the walls and walkways of this market neighbourhood. Rumours began to circulate as to their author's identity but for all his craft and cunning the young man knew that if he were to remain free, then it would be required of him to remain anonymous.

But anonymity is a lonely place so the young man set out to surround himself with trustworthy fellows - a band of merry-men attracted and dedicated to anarchy and activism. A loyal rag-tag band of outlaws and outsiders intent on protecting and serving their newly adopted champion.

```
[Lights dim to show a gang of shadowy figures
clambering across a West London rooftop]
```

Scene 2

```
[Lights come up on an empty stage littered with
spray-cans, stencils and an empty artist's easel]
```

So praised and prolific was our protagonist that he could seemingly do no wrong, but there were taxes to pay and rents to consider and life was costly in the realm of Notting Dale. So along with his troupe of merry-men, he had set out in search of pastures new, wearily settling at the [Ditch-of-Shore] in the eastern reaches of the great metropolis. It was here that they chanced upon an old Inn. The Innkeeper of which was a canny fellow and sensed that the stranger and his troupe might bring good fortune to his ailing business, so had offered them room and board. In return they began to decorate the tired and crumbling walls of his neighbourhood and as before the people had flocked.

```
[Lights dim to show a gang of shadowy figures
clambering across an East London rooftop]
```

Scene 3

```
[Lights come up on a busy and bustling street
scene the walls festooned with vibrant artworks]
```

Very soon, the tired old Inn named after the famed foe of St. George, had become the centre of everything. Robin and his troupe, busying themselves at night in the surrounding streets and by day, creating reproductions of his playful and subversive works to disseminate to his hungry young disciples who had greedily devoured every crumb that fell from his table, hurriedly retreating to their darkened caves like so many rats to sell-on the spoils of their Prophet's labours.

[Lights dim on an East London night scene where dozens of dimly lit windows show hooded and hunched silhouettes working feverishly at their computers]

Act two: TAXES MUST BE PAID

Scene 1

[Lights come up on an empty street scene, one of its walls is obscured by a sinister veil of scaffolding, a thick pall of black dust and smoke emanating from its edges rolls across the stage, as it settles a single figure dressed in black can be seen standing alone stroking his goatee beard and grinning menacingly]

The Sheriff of the Gate of [Notting Hill] who had followed our adventurer and his troupes fortunes and their subsequent rise to fame was determined to get even with his accuser. He had felt slighted and shamed by Robin's insults and his assaults on his integrity had caused great hurt. So being a bearer of grudges he had set out to exact his revenge. He deemed reparation was required to restore order. After all, everyone knows taxes must be paid. So it was, that as Robin and his band of merry-men slept-off the rigours of their nocturnal endeavours, a new sound could be heard throughout the streets and thoroughfares, the piercing whining grind of metal against stone had echoed all about, the baneful wail of injustice as his offerings were torn mercilessly from their place of purpose.

[Lights dim as the black clad figure disappears into a further pall of dense dust and smoke

leaving only the sound of maniacal laughter
echoing around the auditorium]

Scene 2

[Lights come up on a bucolic scene, laid out on
the ground are the broken and abused remnants of
what were once admired monuments to the artist's
celebrity and standing]

The Sheriff had sought the employ of the finest artisans in the land and had charged them with the task of resurrecting and restoring the stolen treasures to their former glory. Over many weeks he had made daily visitations, fretting and fussing as the painstaking process had progressed. The artisans had toiled relentlessly under his watch, working their magic and craft until such time that the Sheriff satisfied at their labours, had paid them their dues and on swearing them to silence on pain of death, had them dismissed. The Sheriff sensing the disquiet and despair his actions had caused had hatched a plan to smuggle the works to a far flung shore in the distant Americas where merchants and marketeers of great wealth did reside. Their purses heavy with gold.

[Lights dim on a chaotic dockside scene a forest
of ships' masts, packing crates and cases
suspended from winches by ropes and chains are
silhouetted against the night sky. Dockhands,
sailors and stevedores busy themselves on the
decks and jetties preparing to set sail. Monkeys
chatter hysterically in the ships rigging as rats
scamper up the mooring ropes]

[Lights come up on a Cathedral-like interior.
Shafts of light from the highest windows piercing
the gloom and highlighting the treasured
collection of works. At its centre, a vast
banqueting table laden with exotic foods and
wines and an enormous candelabrum burning

brightly. The elegant elite begin to fill the room
from both sides of the stage]

The Sheriff had many enemies and his friends were few, but first among them was a tall Hanoverian Prince of fine standing within his community and one whose vision had known no bounds. To house the precious cargo he had built, a stately pleasure dome to which all the most notable and celebrated merchants and grandees were invited. Common folk too, flocked from all about, to stand and stare in awe and wonder at these much feted treasures. Extravagant banquets were held in honour of the works' arrival to their shores. Deals were brokered and covenants settled.

[Lights dim on an empty banqueting table strewn
with the remains of a great feast a pair of
monkeys swing mischievously from the candelabrum
whilst rats forage amid the remnants]

Act three: BETRAYAL

Scene 1

[Lights come up to show a large East London
warehouse its windows blazing brightly through
the dark night sky]

With his street offerings having been savagely ransacked by the Sheriff and his men, there had followed a universal outpouring of grief and rage but Robin's celebrity had continued to grow and grow. The reproductions becoming so popular that a larger premises had been sought to help quench the demand. Crowds would throng excitedly at its doors on the announcement of each new offering. But this new vessel was a leaky one and with his troupe's number now swollen to cope with the clamouring demands of this newfound success, some of its number had succumbed to temptation and as night had fallen, with the presses silenced and the lights extinguished, shadowy figures could be seen weaving ghost like through the buildings corridors, its back door serving as an illicit portal to the nefarious nocturnal workings of a treacherous few.

```
[A completely dark stage is broken by the opening
of a small yet heavy door and in the gloom two
figures can just be made out furtively exchanging
goods for coin, then the door is slammed shut and
the stage returns to darkness]
```

```
Scene 2
```

```
[Lights come up on an empty stage, a hooded figure
sits alone on a simple throne his back to the
audience]
```

Word had come to Robin that some of his [Merry Men] had succumbed to the lure of commerce and that even his most trusted companion and right hand man had betrayed him. His kingdom had become riddled with recalcitrants and rogues interested only in self-aggrandisement and selfish gain. He determined it time to put an end to his followers' errant behaviour and a hurriedly constructed court had been assembled and edicts pronounced, the first decree to banish those who had wronged him from both his court and his kingdom, the second that henceforth and forevermore, he and only he, would have the authority to confirm or denounce a work as being that of his hand or intent and that without his mark or seal would render it quite worthless.

```
[Lights dim silhouetting the solitary figure
abandoned and alone at the heart of his empty
empire, his loyal troupe disbanded, a deity
bereft of his disciples]
```

Scene 3

```
[Lights come up on a palatial interior filled
with a trove of exotic bifurcated taxidermy
```

embellished in silvers and gold. Cabinets of
alchemy and elixirs lining its walls and sat on a
central plinth a tiny jewel encrusted skull. The
room begins to fill with the great and the good
from all of the lands about]

So lauded was our hero that he was courted by all the most important and fashionable figures of the day. People came from miles around to wonder at his offerings and his fame and notoriety grew and grew until such time that his reputation reached the ear of a great and famous [Spot painter] whose influence was without equal. This painter, recognising something of his younger self in this rebellious outsider, had taken him under his wing and over time, had mentored him in the dark arts of commerce and profiteering. His pupil was a keen study and before long the windows of his warehouse were once again blazing through the night. But this time, the back door had been sealed shut. There were to be no more leaks and furthermore, it was decreed that all past impressions be brought to book in-front of a select jury of loyal followers and their self-anointed King. Documents bearing his mark and seal were to be issued judicially and punitively, old allegiances ignored, past friendships crushed. Fortunes made. The hopeful young man that had set out to make a name for himself all those years ago had indeed done just that and that name was BANKSY.

[Lights dim silhouetting a faux castle nestling
in the West Hollywood Hills a solitary figure sat
in an ivory tower. A King in his counting house
counting out his money]

[Curtain comes down]

STAR CAST

Boy from Bristol - Banksy

Sheriff of the Gate of [Notting Hill] - Robin Barton

Hanoverian Prince - Stephan Keszler

The Spot Painter - Damien Hirst

Robin's Merry Men

Steven Lazarides, Ben Eine, Holly Cushing, Simon Durban, Jo Brooks

OTHER CAST MEMBERS

Robin Birley	Rochelle Godden
Jon Bon Jovi	Keith Allen
Andrew Lamberty	Sky Grimes
Roger DeHaan	Alastair Upton

EPILOGUE

EPILOGUE

Wiping away the greasepaint of another villainous performance and with the jeering, mocking applause, still ringing in my ears, I had paused to consider how very different things might have been had I not spent that long ago summer of 1977 sat at the bar of the Black Swan in the county of Warwickshire. Its walls littered with a mosaic of autographed portraits of the celebrated thespians who had trodden the boards of its nearby theatre, who had sought succour within the pub's sacred walls. Back then I had imagined myself part of their troupe, one of their own, an insider sharing in their celebrity, absorbing the gossip and glamour that they represented. I had spent one half of a lifetime trying to recreate that sense of belonging which I had felt during that formative summer. But celebrity and fame had continued to evade and disappoint me. I had brushed shoulders with 'the great and the good' from the worlds of music, fashion, literature and art but had never really been invited in - kept waiting like a tradesman at the door. Always on the outside, looking in.

I had been 'Robin Banksy' now for twelve years but had become weary, not of the charade but of the blind devotion that my nemesis had inspired. I told myself it wasn't jealousy but injustice which had been my motivation. I had no interest in unmasking our pantomime hero, rather to silence the sanctimonious bleating of his tedious acolytes. For almost two decades his every endeavour had been met with fervent and slavish excitement. Each humble offering receiving platitudinous praise and applause on its release, only to be flipped for profit and gain by his greedy, ungracious disciples and in doing so, creating and maintaining a cycle of self-serving gluttony. A perilous game of 'Pass the Parcel' wherein each new recipient risked being the holder when the music stopped.

But the music hadn't stopped. The parcel was still being passed and with the artist's star still firmly in its ascendance, I had decided it was time to bow-out gracefully, to allow our latter-day Robin Hood his day. Besides, I was losing my appetite for the task. It's true, I had relished and revelled in my role as the villain of the piece - a carefully curated and absurd vaudevillian character full of pomp and impropriety. But it had been the hypocrisy that launched me onto this stage, had spurred me on and it was that same hypocrisy which remained - despite my best efforts to shine a light on the greed and excess that lay at the heart of the artist's empire.

His controlling nature, which had locked-out those closest to him and banished those who had dared to stand against him, had guaranteed him a place in art history. But it was the mean-spirited manipulation of the media and the ruthless hard-fought and fiercely protected anonymity which had proved the real key to his success. Ironically, it was that same key which had proved his Achilles' heel. The key that which allowed me to unlock plunder and parade his much lauded artworks with complete impunity. The stage set, its players readied, its scripts studied, its lines learned.

'Robin the artist would put his celebrated offerings out onto the streets to the joy of the people who would throng enthusiastically about. Robin the thief would avail himself of the offering making it his own for the gain of profit. Robin the artist would make known his fury at this action but his anonymity rendered him impotent. Robin the thief would make known his indifference to the artist's ire and so the cycle would perpetuate.

But the show, that had run for more than a decade, was looking increasingly absurd. A forty-five-year-old Rebel under the patronage of a fifty-five-year-old Spot Painter. Pitched against a sixty-two-year-old foe, who should have known better. What had begun life as a work of urban derring-do and cunning had turned into an all too predictable pantomime of manners, a West End hit reduced to little more than a seedy seaside farce.

Waiting in the wings on that, the final night's performance, I could hear the taunting and mocking chants of 'Banksy Banksy Banksy!!!' emanating from the half-empty auditorium. The sound which had served as my cue for so many years. To each player then, a final bow before the curtain falls, a last retort, a final thought.

Were it not for my Robin Banksy, when Banksy was robin' you, who had really been Robin who?

[audience]

He's behind you!!!....oh no he's not!!

SHIP OF FOOLS

SHIP OF FOOLS

At some point in the early part of the last decade a coastal haar had come off the sea above Kent and had crept silently and slowly up the river Thames. Rolling past the silenced trading rooms of the city's financial district, onward, past the drowning posts and opium dens of Limehouse, past Traitors' Gate and on still, beyond the hanging fields of Tower Hill.

A yellow murky miasma which had concealed within, a ghostly flotilla of golden galleon, crewed by a ragtag bunch of avaricious cheats and chancers, fallen foul of the financial regulators. Debarred and precluded from the trading floors, they had set sail, in search of oceans new.

Finally dropping anchor in a neglected Mayfair backwater, peering through the fog-bound doorways and windows of the neighbourhood's august institutions, there could be seen the sleepy denizens of an art world caught slumbering. Anaesthetised and torpid, the bloated burghers of a bourgeoisie made lazy through inactivity and sloth.

The crew, having scuppered their vessels and cut their lines, had set about hijacking and reshaping this tired and moribund industry to suit their needs - and had busied themselves with finessing their craft. They had quickly established that the skill-sets honed on the trading floors of yore, if applied with cunning, zeal and zest, could yield remarkable revenue and results.

The last truly unregulated market could provide a platform for the greatest Ponzi scheme ever created. Like the pharaohs before them, they would build a magnificent pyramid. Not in the deserts of Egypt but in the very heart of Mayfair, a monument to Mammon, its foundations fashioned not of stone but greed. The fusty clan of overseers who had been caught napping could do little more than look on in despair, their hands shackled by colonial manners and mediocrity.

Hastily constructed trading temples had sprung up seemingly overnight. An intoxicating fog now hung permanently over this already opulent and extravagant neighbourhood, a fog that seemed to obscure any sense of truth or decency. Gaudy baubles flashed ostentatiously from out of the gloom, hinting at riches within reach. Circus tents were hurriedly erected in the squares and parks to cater for the growing crowds.

Not since the 'May Fairs' of old had the neighbourhood witnessed such scenes. Clamour and excitement spilled out onto its avenues and squares. Fame-hungry hordes vied to gain access to the parties and previews. Paparazzi prowled the pavements, hunting and haranguing their prey in chase of profit. Newly opened elite private clubs promised sanctuary from prying eyes, sanctums in which members could gorge themselves with impunity, where parody grotesques could roam freely, from table to table, preening and parading their wealth in a dizzying and disorienting game of musical chairs.

The shroud of fog, pierced not by the celestial summit of a sun-soaked pyramid of promise but instead by the jagged tip of an iceberg that bellied what lay beneath. A dark brooding cesspit of debt, growing incrementally with each rogue trade. The respectable veneer of the polished picture palaces, which served as the shop fronts to these frontiersman, swindlers, fraudsters and mountebanks, disguising their true purpose. Sideshow barkers, dressed in sharp suits, coaxing and cajoling the wealthy with promises of quick profits and instant returns, preying on the ignorant and uneducated. Tic-tac touts relying on wristwatch etiquette to inform and opine.

As the fog had begun to clear and the tide of greed had gently receded, the faintly etched rigging of a solitary craft could be made out against the retreating yellow pallor, in its wake lay a golden galleon washed up on the shores of Mayfair.

A ship of fools emptied of its rag-tag crew, a beautiful and abandoned monument to an ugly era of avarice. Its extravagant dark crimson interior, a testament to a time when cash had been king.

An empty vessel representing the futility of ignorance. Looted, left high and dry, its cargo of bullion vanished, its rivals vanquished. The dizzying and disorienting feeding-frenzy finished, the battle-deck malcontents having moved on, leaving the now deserted squares of Mayfair littered with the detritus of the turned tide, a tired and forlorn landscape. Its museums and mansions ghostly quiet, mawkish mausoleums to Mammon.

Hanging heavy in the air, the deafening hush that had followed the failed coup. The bandit gangs of parakeets silenced, disappeared and disavowed. The hysteria evaporated. The sky blue.

To the northern end of Berkeley Square a young girl holding a red heart-shaped balloon trips giddily down the steps of an abandoned and boarded-up auction house. Skipping playfully amid the park's Plane trees, aimlessly running a stick along the square's iron railings, the rhythmic rat-a-tat-tat piercing the silence, stopping suddenly to stare down at the paved stones beneath her feet, then hopping excitedly from one square to another. A gentle gust tugs impishly, freeing the string from her grasp. The girl watches the balloon's wistful ascent as the plaintive call of a lone nightingale sings out.

When two lovers meet in Mayfair, so the legends tell,
Songbirds sing; winter turns to spring.
Every winding street in Mayfair falls beneath the spell.

A Nightingale Sang in Berkeley Square - Maschwitz/Sherwin

...TWO YEARS LATER...

A FOOL AND HIS MONEY

A FOOL AND HIS MONEY

The auctioneers gavel came down with a pistol like report that woke me abruptly from my trance like state, the room erupted with gasps and wild applause!!

"Hi it's Daniel.. Daniel Boffey," said the voice. "From the Guardian newspaper."

I was no fan of this particular periodical but in this instance I had had an almost allergic reaction to this measured introduction. He went on to explain that a Liverpool street artist working under the moniker of 'Silent Bill' had claimed authorship of a work titled 'Never Liked This Banksy' and he was inviting me, somewhat archly, if I would like to comment on this assertion. Like a cat playing with a wounded mouse, he was enjoying (rather too much) the ensuing silence.

What we both knew then and know now, was that this was a cruelly rhetorical question on his part and one that would unravel in a vicious cyclone of lies accusations and half-truths. The facts as they were laid out, were simple and straightforward: A work attributed to the artist known as Banksy had been included in a television auction and the pilot production filmed over five days at a warehouse in an achingly fashionable East London enclave. The show's working title 'The Greatest Auction' had boasted an extravaganza of unparalleled opulence and intrigue, featuring items sourced from around the globe, by a skilled and inquisitive team of researchers and it was to this ferment I had arrived in the spring of 2023.

I had come to the attention of the show's creators through the pages of my social media, a mendacious collection of self-serving narcissistic nonsense... but one that had absorbed much of my waking (and non-waking) hours since my retreat from the glare of adverse publicity from my past antics. I had grown weary of the constant criticism and the damning onslaughts from the popular press. Like a duelist, his blade had been blunted in battle I had decided to throw down my sword and return to my castle on the coast.

But the call inviting me to participate in this proposed series had been just too tempting to ignore. My only surprise, I had reflected, was that it had taken so long for my nascent skills to be recognised. Surely after all, my carefully crafted social-media self, that I had worked at so meticulously in the fallow months following my self-imposed exile would simply and seamlessly transfer to 'Real Life'. Fortuitously I had recently been given the opportunity to host a series of filmed interviews at a 15th Century Inn, a darkly atmospheric, near invisible hideaway historically favoured by local smugglers, thieves and highwaymen. I had chanced upon the Lantern Inn one Sunday when returning from a sortie on the south Kent coast and had been thrilled to discover that the proprietor was one Andy Blake a six foot four piratical punk who I had first met some four decades earlier. We had immediately bonded and when a location had been sought for filming his was the obvious choice.

Formatted as the 'Lantern Lunches' these were to be one on one discussions exploring a number of topics pertinent to the much hyped Web3 space, a notional shangri-la, a utopian haven, devoid of the pedantry of taxes and regulations, a 'Welcome mat' to the Metaverse and its terrestrial heartland - DUBAI.

"Dubai pal its the f*cking future, I'm telling you pal" so my longtime friend and collaborator Patrick was telling me (his rabid enthusiasm tripping from his tongue at breakneck speed) he was on a now all-too-familiar evangelical rant as to the benefits of his newly discovered utopia. In stark contrast, we were in an empty car park in Canterbury Kent, our brace of black Range Rover's parked back to back as he was energetically moving thirty odd cling film wrapped packages from one vehicle to the other. To a passing onlooker it might well have resembled a scene from a scouse version of Narcos, whereas the truth was way more fantastical. The contents of these sinister looking packages were in fact what had remained of the "painstakingly" rescued Banksy artwork known as 'Love Plane'. Featuring a vast hand sprayed Heart formed of a smoke trail emanating from an old-fashioned biplane. The work, originally sited on the flank wall of a multistorey car park opposite the Liverpool War Museum, had been victim to many attacks and incursions since its arrival, with the biplane having been physically removed some six years earlier, leaving its disenfranchised message of hope to languish largely unnoticed, but on the news of the building's imminent demolition a team had been hastily pulled together, tasked with the heart's removal.

It was true that this would be no mean feat - with the work measuring some four meters in height. Undeterred, the team had enthusiastically embraced the task, armed only with hammers and chisels they had worked tirelessly through the night but as dawn had broken

it was clear that lack of instruction and any real plan had resulted in the pockmarked wall looking like something out of 1980's Beirut. Proud as punch, the team had sent enthusiastic video updates throughout the night but over the ensuing hours it became apparent they hadn't really understood the intricacies of the task.. to salvage not destroy!!

"Dubai pal its the f*cking future, I'm telling you pal" he had repeated as the last package was added to the ramshackle pile straining the Range's air suspension to its limit. On arriving at my restorers the following day I had felt the pang of anguish as the packages were unfurled revealing hundreds of shards of mangled masonry, the cardiothoracic rigour required to rebuild this particular broken heart would clearly require unparalleled patience.

At some point between the biplanes earlier extraction and the heart's recent removal, a new work had mysteriously appeared at the base of the wall, featuring a small rat brandishing a paintbrush having recently daubed the words 'NEVER LIKED THIS BANKSY' in red. I had expressed some doubt as to the veracity of the work but regardless, it was decided to take the piece just in case. Quite how the work found its way from its Liverpudlian waste-ground to 'The Greatest auction' catalogue is open to debate but there it was..

Lot no.11 'NEVER LIKED THIS BANKSY' critically with the caveat "Attributed to Banksy".

It was clear from the get-go that my role in the show was to act as one of the star bidders, and with my history and reputation I was the obvious choice to lead the bidding on this particular lot.

On the day of the sale, we had filed into the carefully curated viewing room, where we were invited to pass comment on the work. I had been immediately struck by the similarity to an earlier Banksy work titled 'NEVER LIKED THE BEATLES' that I had successfully sold two decades earlier but something felt wrong, why would the famously diffident artist make comment on his own work, it was at the very least uncharacteristic. But I had considered if I were to build on my television career this was no time for procrastination. Perhaps after all it was no longer for me to prove a work was by Banksy rather the onus should be on him to deny a work. In the absence of any denial, I had concluded I would be prepared to take a punt on it.. after all I had told myself, where could be the harm in it.

For my part I had been woefully unprepared for the hysteria unleashed by my actions on that day. To my mind the performance had been faultless and come the hour I had excelled, having brazenly etched my maximum bid with a black sharpie onto the palm of my hand. Dressed in a Mark Powell midnight blue three piece suit, hands adorned with a sparkling array of Stephen Webster's finest, I had stepped into the arena with only one ambition and that ambition.. TO WIN!!

The auctioneers gavel came down with a pistol like report that woke me abruptly from my trance like state, the room erupted with gasps and wild applause!!

The winning bid a tidy £250,000 pounds, the exact amount revealed on my extended palm. My doubters and haters would surely be silenced by this brazen show of strength, I had won not just the bid but the show. But even as I bathed in the immediate glory of this gladiatorial achievement, I had sensed dark murmurings from the shadows, my haters rather than being silenced had clearly been incensed by my arrogant performance. Accusations of double dealing had reached the ears of the show's producers and I had found myself interrogated at length over accusations of duplicity. The light hearted game show atmosphere of 'The Greatest Auction' had transformed into what felt like a probing episode of 'Panorama' and overnight a kangaroo court had been put in place, the spurious charge at its heart being that I had been both seller and buyer and as such had breached, if not the rules of auction then certainly the spirit of those rules.

The production company, rattled by the press revelations and the presumption of double-dealing, had been quick to condemn, conveniently forgetting it was they who had corralled the team of bidders on that fateful day. I had bid in good faith against an unseen adversary and had won but it was a hollow victory and one set to haunt me.

Rules be damned!!.. I had thought but I was clearly alone in this assertion. The press and the forums were gleeful in their condemnation. Whilst behind the scenes the talk was of duplicity and double dealing, in the public realm it was all about 'a fool and his money'... how dare this arrogant interloper throw his money around with such abandon! money no doubt earned by nefarious means, money that could have been better spent on good causes, a bewildering and bizarre sentiment considering it was, at least on the face of it, my money! Suddenly it was as if I was expected to be some kind of philanthropist, rather than the greedy, freewheeling self-serving marketeer that I clearly was.

With the fallout and collateral damage caused by my very public display of arrogance and avarice still swirling about me. I was forced to accept that my television career was over before it had started. Once again I had flown too close to the sun and had paid the price. Bruised but not broken, I had been preparing to retreat into the comfort of my social media malaise, when a message had popped up on my phone.

"Hi Robin.. We've never met, but after a bit of research I've come across your details, and I am hoping that you may be able to assist me with something"

It transpired that on the night of the show's inaugural episode, across town the managing director of a well-known construction company had settled-in for the evening and scrolling through the channels had chanced upon a new Chanel 4 pilot in which the British actor Hugh Bonneville's narration was calmly introducing a sharply besuited individual with more rings than fingers, sporting dark glasses the character was striding purposefully through a graffiti-strewn wasteland..

"Robin Barton aka Bankrobber is an art dealer specialising in Banksy Street Works".

In the immediate aftermath of Silent Bill's revelation, he'd bathed in the glory bestowed upon him by the local press, an overnight sensation, a working class David to my much vilified Goliath. Within days however, the perceived burden of wealth had overwhelmed him and to his cohorts he was just another sold-out street artist, a traitor to his tribe.. A RICH KID.

SHOP 'TIL YOU DROP

SHOP 'TIL YOU DROP

Over the past twelve years I had regularly made the journey along the length of Bruton Lane. The dark snaking thoroughfare linking Bruton Street to the southernmost reaches of Berkeley Square, a dilapidated corridor littered with service access points and parked-up trade vehicles.... but at the northern end of this cut-through had resided a treasure - the holy grail! Banksy's monumental 'Shop 'Til You Drop' - a magnificent monochrome iteration depicting the silhouette of a young woman in free-fall, desperately clinging to a shopping trolley, a solitary bottle of champagne and string of pearls spilling out before her. Plummeting to imminent oblivion, a comment on consumerism.

The artwork had survived unscathed and largely unnoticed for more than a decade but its prescient message remained as relevant today as it had on the day of its creation, applied some thirty-foot from ground level in the very heart of a neighborhood bloated by greed. Daily line-ups of impossibly young aspirational shoppers, waiting patiently for the latest offerings from the gods of fashion; Saint Laurent, Chanel, Prada, Gucci, Louis Vuitton... blacked-out chariots of the uber-rich, gliding past with comforting regularity. A terrestrial testament to wealth.

And it was to this, the playground of the rich, on a cold November morning in the year of 2011 that two men arrived in white overalls and could be seen unloading a van, subsequently erecting a ten-meter-tall scaffolding tower, shrouded in protective white tarpaulin, behind which, a shadowy figure at work.

By the end of the following day all that had remained of the collective visit was Banksy's message.

Produced just five days prior to the annual shopping extravaganza known as 'Black Friday' and three years on from Sotheby's 'Beautiful Inside My Head Forever' a two-day sale that had netted the artist Damien Hirst a staggering £111m. Art and commerce blurring incoherently in a vortex of venality.

The canvas to Banksy's falling shopper was a neglected, stark grey, granite-faced, office block squeezed uncomfortably onto a narrow triangle of land behind New Bond Street... at its widest point, opening onto Mayfair's Grafton Street and at its narrowest, the 'The Coach & Horses' pub on Bruton Street, a 'Tudorbethan' coaching Inn that had served as a retreat from my travails on many occasions.

I don't recall when I had first become aware of the work's arrival but with its proximity to my beloved Berkeley Square and the magnetic draw of New Bond Street, with its auction houses and grandiose galleries, it had become something of an obsession. Rarely a day had gone by over a twelve year tenure that I hadn't imagined myself taking control of its fate. I had regularly wrestled with the logistics of how best she might be rescued from the wrath of the wrecking ball. On two occasions I had felt her within my reach but every time the trail had gone cold and I'd reluctantly accepted that her fate was now firmly outside of my influence.

The last time I had seen her falling form, she was cloaked behind that wall of scaffold and tarpaulin (in birth, as in death) and I felt certain this would be my last sight of her. For two days straight I bore witness to the baleful whining sound of steel on stone but on a rain-riven Monday morning, I'd turned off Bruton Street into the familiar cut-through and I had been struck by a sudden sense of absence. Not only had the now familiar skeleton of scaffolding vanished... so had the entire building, raised to the ground in less than 48 hours.

Although I had known of the planned demolition for some time, the brutal manner and swiftness of execution hit me hard. I hadn't been prepared for the sense of loss that subsequently haunted me in the ensuing weeks.

When a familiar building, one etched indelibly on the psyche, is erased so abruptly, the temptation is to try and hold its memory to place like mercury striking glass, but the absence was both immediate and permanent, no psycho-geographic imprint - just an empty void. My hopes and plans for the piece (which I had boasted-of over so many years) had ultimately come to nothing. The willful destruction of this, the holy grail of Banksy's street work, had left me feeling downcast and disillusioned. However, fate can be a fickle foe and in a simple twist, it transpired that my appearance on a recent calamitous TV auction show (the screening of which had caused me so much discomfort) was ironically set to turn the tide in my favour.

Just as I had been preparing to retreat into the cloistered comfort of my social media world, the author of a random text, received some weeks earlier, showed his hand. He was (he explained) the contractor tasked with the demolition of the properties situated at 22-24 Bruton Lane ahead of redevelopment into a luxury hotel and office complex. As such, he had taken control of a Banksy artwork known as 'Shop 'Til You Drop' that had stood at the site. He went on to explain that he had watched my appearance on the show and immediately instructed his assistant to track me down.. "Three clicks and your it!"

Remarkably, the work not only survived the demolition, it had remained entirely intact. A magnificent ten ton, four-meter-square monolith. The artist's message unwavering in its intent, Its fate..

"Robin Barton aka Bankrobber is an art dealer specialising in Banksy Street Works".

[SHOP 'TIL YOU DROP] Stencil & Spray Paint on stone - Price £10,000,000

Printed in Great Britain
by Amazon